NEVER TO BE FREE

Books by Josef Carl Grund

YOU HAVE A FRIEND, PIETRO
BEYOND THE BRIDGE
NEVER TO BE FREE

NEVER
TO BE FREE
A Novel by
Josef Carl Grund

Translated by Lucile Harrington

LITTLE, BROWN AND COMPANY

BOSTON   TORONTO

LIBRARY OF CONGRESS CATALOG CARD NO. 79-91226

FIRST EDITION

*Published simultaneously in Canada
by Little, Brown & Company (Canada) Limited*

PRINTED IN THE UNITED STATES OF AMERICA

THESE CHILDREN will learn nothing except to think German, to act German, and when the boys are ten years old they will go into the Hitler Youth organization. There we will keep them for four years, and then we will not give them back but take them directly into the Party, into the Work Force, into the Storm Troop, the Home Defense Squad, or the Motor Corps, and so on. And if in two years or two and a half they have not become wholly National Socialists, then they will go into the Labor Service and will be drilled for six or seven months with one implement: the German spade. And any class consciousness or pride which may still exist here and there will be dealt with by the Army for two years, and so that there will be no chance of back-sliding, after two, three, or four years, we will take them again into the Storm Troop or the Home Defense, and so on, and they will never be free again for their whole lives.

—Hitler, 1938

NEVER TO BE FREE

✠ 1 ✠

Once Upon a Time

ONCE UPON A TIME — but this is not a fairy story; it is harsh, bloody reality.

Twenty years ago, Sunday, October 1, 1944. My father's convalescent leave was coming to an end, and he, Mother and I were making the most of every minute. At twelve past one the train of First Lieutenant Hermann Briel would leave — direction, east. Until then each moment was worth three.

Unfortunately Dad's wound was healed, and now every man was needed at the Front. He belonged to us for only three hours more. To me especially. Yesterday I had received the order to report for active duty. After tomorrow I would no longer be a student; I would be Antiaircraft Gunner Briel. A soldier like my father.

Here at home, as well as at the Front, men were

needed. With increasing frequency British and American planes were bombing German cities. For a long time now the word hinterland had not meant security. Our city had not been spared, although the air attacks had been directed chiefly at the railroad stations and industrial plants. It was bad for those who lived near these targets.

Since the summer of 1944 we had had total war, proclaimed by Goebbels in Berlin and greeted by his audience with rousing cheers. I was for it, too. The English and Americans would find out what stuff we were made of!

Some weeks before our V-1 rocket had flown to London, and the British had retaliated with terror attacks on our cities. Up to that time the part of the city in which we lived had been spared. I had only heard from the safety of our air-raid shelter the deep roar of the enemy's four-engined bombers, the dull banging of the antiaircraft guns, and the screaming explosions of the bombs. But I had seen the horrors they left behind. After each attack I had helped to clear away the rubble and rescue the victims. And each time I was so overcome with rage that I longed for the chance to strike back.

Now it had come. Four days before, our school

had been closed. Several months earlier boys and girls in the two upper classes had received their assignments as *flakhelfers* or assistants in antiaircraft emplacements, as workers in munitions factories, public transportation, military hospitals and, in the case of those about to graduate, as soldiers at the Front. When the school closed, the younger students were evacuated to the country where they would be safer. Their teachers went with them so that their school work could continue.

We sixteen-year-old boys remained. We were needed at the antiaircraft guns. I was proud to be regarded as a man, capable like a true Hitler youth of becoming swift as a greyhound, tough as leather, hard as steel, eager for the soldier's life, firmly resolved to look after myself. When the final victory came, I wanted to be there in the big parade, not to hail the victors, but to be hailed the victorious warrior. Perhaps I might even win a medal — the Iron Cross, Second Class or at least the Military Cross of Merit.

"I won't disgrace you, Dad," I promised.

"It would be no disgrace if you refused," he answered.

"Not one of us will refuse!" I protested. "In the

Hitler Youth we have had the best premilitary training. We have shot the newest type of rifle, we can handle pistols and know how to adapt ourselves to terrain. We can stand up to quite a lot, you'd better believe!"

"All right then. Let's take our bearings." He opened the atlas and marked the front line on the map of Europe with pins. Strong enemy forces had penetrated Holland and were threatening Germany on the northwest flank. In the west big American tank units were pushing forward. At Dunkirk on the English Channel our artillery was engaged in a difficult defensive action. The front line in the south ran from the Western Alps through Central Italy to the bend in the Danube on both sides of the iron gate of the Balkans.

In the east Soviet troops had got to the passes of Ostbeskiden and the Bay of Riga. Warsaw was burning. In Finland German units were fighting a defensive battle against an enemy superior in numbers. Enemy bombers and pursuit planes had strafed the region along the left bank of the Rhine and attacked Karlsruhe on the right.

This was the situation according to the last army despatch. As my father marked it out on the map, he muttered, "The encirclement gets narrower day by day."

"And the number of victims increases," Mother added.

"On both sides!" I said defiantly. "Before we're through, the others will pay for this!"

Father stood looking out the window. "The others do not have to rely on greenhorns," he remarked.

That was too much! I wanted to make an angry retort; then it dawned on me why he said it. Man, don't you understand anything, Gustav? Dad is testing you. Pull yourself together.

Why hadn't I caught on immediately? My father was a member of the party* and wore the Iron Cross, both First and Second Class. I smiled and said, "If Hitler thinks we are worthy to defend the country, we aren't greenhorns. Hitler always does the right thing!"

I really meant it; I had never heard anything else. They all said it — the teachers in school, the leaders in the Hitler Youth, the men of the party, and scores of banners: "The Führer is always right!"

* The National Socialist party, of which Hitler was the Führer (leader).

7

My father persisted. "At the Front, things look very different from the way they do in your training classes, my boy."

Now really, I thought, you are kidding me. "No enemy will set his foot on German soil except as a prisoner!" I shouted. I had heard this, too, in the Hitler Youth school. "And when the Führer gives the order for the secret weapon to be used —"

My father interrupted. "The V-1 and V-2 flew against London weeks ago."

"They are only the beginning, Dad!"

"And what, in your opinion, is the secret weapon like, Gustav?"

Even this question didn't disturb me. In school and in the Hitler Youth sessions we had often debated it. The adults also expected that the secret weapon would be used when the crisis came. That would be in a very short time, just when the enemy believed he was very close to victory. Although no one knew what the weapon was really like, it was possible to guess.

"Perhaps there are death rays which will make every enemy plane crash as soon as it approaches our borders, Dad."

"Too good to be true," Mother said bitterly. She was blowing the same horn as my father! I was getting all mixed up. They should not carry it so far.

"Or a gigantic bomb which could at once wipe out an entire city and cause a conflagration too awful to imagine. Or —" I broke off when neither of them nodded in agreement.

"Anyway, it will be something so dreadful it will bring the enemy to his knees!"

Father and Mother exchanged a quick look. "All right, son, let's leave it. Look out for yourself and don't be ashamed if you do get frightened. Fear is not cowardice. I was terrified before the battle in which I won the first Iron Cross. Defend yourself as well as you can — and don't lose your head if you find some day that it's all very different from what you imagine now."

"I don't know what you mean."

"It doesn't matter, Gustav. Keep your eyes and ears open, and don't get upset if another person says something contrary to your ideas. Many a one who does not think as we do can be an upright man."

"And many a one who roars *Sieg Heil** can be a scoundrel," Mother added.

"Enough of this," my father decided. "Let's talk about something else." So we discussed trivial matters, but I was not really paying attention. My parents were unlike their usual selves, yet I still thought perhaps they were only testing me. On the other hand, were the things they said intended as a warning? If so, a warning of what? Were they afraid to speak too clearly?

Mother called us to dinner. She had prepared a feast. Heaven knows how she had managed to get these scarce delicacies — certainly not with our small allotment of ration stamps.

After dinner we walked to the station. A number of bombs had hit it, but the tracks had been repaired. My father embraced us both. "Bring the Knight's Cross when you come back again!" I said, deliberately cheerful.

"Above all, come back, Hermann!" Mother begged. He waved to us and disappeared in the crowd.

"When Dad returns, he'll certainly be a cap-

* "Hail to the victory!"

1 0

tain," I said to Mother, "or do you think they'll make him a major?"

But what had come over her? "Hold your tongue!" she scolded, then rushed so rapidly through the crowd that I had trouble keeping up with her.

✠ 2 ✠

October 2, 1944

I LEFT HOME at half-past seven. Promptly at eight we stood in ranks in the school yard, three rows with four boys in each, most of them in Hitler Youth uniform.

There were fifteen boys and seventeen girls in our class. Now just twelve of the fifteen boys were lined up: three were missing, not from cowardice or because they wanted to shirk a duty. Peter Rennert had been in the hospital for several weeks. In the last bombing his street had been struck. The cellar in which he had taken refuge was demolished, and a steel girder had crushed his right leg. It had to be amputated.

Max Engelmann had contracted a severe lung inflammation, and Rainer Benkert was not fit to be a soldier. He had been sickly ever since we had known him.

Our school had gotten off with only slight damage, just a bomb crater in the school yard. It was in this yard that we lined up: twelve students of the sixth class in the Classical High School.

Long Bayer was on the right flank: Franz Bayer, six feet three inches tall, thin as a rake, the best running high jumper in the school, fresh as they come. What could shake him hadn't yet been discovered. "If you're going to get caught, you're going to get caught whether you hide or not" was his slogan. He had a girl friend; many of us admired him for this; I was more impressed by his coolness than by his interest in girls.

Near Long Bayer stood Helmut Schroeder, a typical grind. I didn't like him; he boasted too much about honors for which he had no right to take credit. "My father is a lieutenant colonel," or "My brother has received the Iron Cross, First Class," or "My mother was an opera singer; she knows the Führer personally." Just because of Schroeder I wished that my father might receive the Knight's Cross since that was a degree above

1 3

the Iron Cross. The big shot couldn't beat that. The Knight's Cross of a first lieutenant or captain would outweigh a lieutenant colonel and an opera singer ten times over!

Willi Braun: We called him Barbarossa because he had red hair and already needed to shave. The best of pals — always on the spot where anything crazy was going on. Once when the Latin teacher left the key on the outside of the teachers' lavatory, Barbarossa locked the door. The prisoner roared for almost a quarter of an hour, not in Latin, but in very forceful German, until the biology teacher freed him. We never found out who squealed on Barbarossa. If the Hitler Youth leader had not spoken for him, he would have been expelled.

Alfred Schmidt: The head of the class, but only in school. His single poor mark was in gym, as you might guess by looking at him. His shoulders were stooped; when standing at attention he looked more like a question mark than a soldier. Besides, he was timid. During the first air raid on our city he had been buried in an air-raid shelter for five hours. He could not forget it. But as a classmate he was all right. I owed him many passing marks on Latin assignments. Not that he had given me private lessons; he slipped me notes in class.

Karl Korner: We called him "the Bull." He had won the school championship eight times boxing against a heavyweight. And in other ways he'd bang his head against the wall. When he wanted to convince someone, he did it better with fists than with arguments. In Greek he stood easily at the foot of the class. He loved to eat; anyone who slipped him some food in this time of shortages was his friend. Korner was happy about becoming a soldier in the first line because there he could get second helpings — so an infantryman had told him.

Gustav Adolf Briel: That was I. My friends called me Gabriel, although Long Bayer said, "You are as much like an angel as a mouse is like a horse."

Josef Schneider: We called him "the brave little tailor."* That wasn't a joke; we said it with a good deal of respect. He wore the Military Cross of Merit on his Hitler Youth uniform. The district leader had presented it to him after the second air attack on the city, when he had rescued a thirteen-

* Schneider means tailor in German.

year-old boy from a burning house. None of us, except perhaps Schroeder, grudged him the honor. Schneider himself made nothing of it and let the medal speak for itself.

Manfred Huber: He wanted to be a professional soldier and become at least a general. "Graduates get on the General Staff more easily than drop-outs," he declared, and plugged away at his studies although he found the going hard. In rifle practice he was ahead of all the rest of us.

Otto Thumser: His father was a staff doctor at the Front, and Otto dreamed of sometime becoming a famous surgeon. He was something of a loner, played the piano in his free time, loved Bach and Beethoven but not Wagner. He never pushed himself forward, but he was there when you needed him.

Walter Müller: He was my friend, chiefly because he was so good at listening. Even when he contradicted, he did it in such an agreeable way that you couldn't get angry with him. Besides, he had a sister Karin, fifteen years old.

Fritz Hauschild: We called him Bubi. Karl Korner had heard his mother use that pet name, and it stuck. Bubi stormed and raved like a lunatic to no avail. He was a born firebrand, could fly into a rage over the smallest thing and take on boys much stronger than he. He never seemed to mind the beatings he got. He would probably be capable of rushing against an armored tank with his bare fists. (This idea came, naturally, from Long Bayer, and Bubi, also naturally, had flung himself on the joker, who towered two heads over him.)

Hartmut Gerngross: He was "the little one." I could not figure him out very well. He was in the Hitler Youth, performed his duties like everyone else, yet if anyone reviled the priests or the "Jewish swine" he would turn away and leave. "The cub with the sensitive soul," Schroeder had mocked, until Long Bayer cut him short.

"Guess what! I burned my Latin books in the corner, Gabriel," grinned Bull, who was standing near me. Alfred Schmidt poked him in the side. "Shut up, they're coming!"

Long Bayer stepped forward and barked, "Company, attention!" We clicked our heels and stood rigid. "For the report to the headmaster, eyes left!" Eleven heads turned. Franz Bayer marched to the headmaster, halted, and announced, "Twelve students of the sixth class lined up!"

We called our headmaster Zeus, not that he had anything in common with the Greek god, but because he was the chief of the education division. The golden party badge on his lapel impressed us more than his position. His bald head gleamed like a mirror, he was painfully thin, and spoke in a falsetto. Behind Zeus stood the leader of our Hitler Youth Corps and a lieutenant of the antiaircraft artillery.

Zeus raised his hand in salute. "Thank you, Bayer. Rejoin the formation." Then he turned to us. "*Heil*, comrades!"

"*Heil*, Headmaster!"

"At ease!"

We stood left foot forward, arms hanging loosely. Zeus had called us comrades! What a distinction! I was tremendously proud. "How times change," growled Barbarossa from the third row so that only we could hear him. "Comrades! A few months ago he called me a blockhead!"

"Shut up!" Schroeder hissed.

"Comrades!" Zeus cried out again, and drew

himself up. "In a few hours you will be wearing the uniform of soldiers. Prove yourselves worthy of it and of your school. I may be standing before you for the last time, and this is farewell. I have had my teacher's exemption canceled and have applied for service at the Front. I must settle my account. To all of you much luck, and may you come back in good health. For the Führer and the Generals of the Armed Forces —"

We clicked our heels and raised our arms in the Nazi salute.

"A three times *Sieg!*" Zeus shouted.

"*Heil!*" we roared back. "*Sieg! Heil! Sieg! Heil!*"

Zeus turned to the corps leader. "You will take over the rest."

"Yes, Sir. May I have permission to say that I admire you?"

Zeus shook his head. "No, we'll let that go."

After shaking hands with the corps leader and the lieutenant, he left. The corps leader looked so serious that none of us moved. We had never seen him like that before; usually he ridiculed any show of emotion, but something between Zeus and him must have affected him personally.

The door through which Zeus had left swung to. "Four days ago the headmaster received word that his son had fallen in action on the western front," the corps leader said. "He is going now to take his place. Let your teacher be an example to you, comrades! Rate your own lives cheap, if it comes to that, and remember, a German knows no fear. I wish you courage, German loyalty, and soldiers' luck!"

I had never cared much for Zeus as a teacher, but now I was all for him. His attitude was exactly right, in my opinion.

The corps leader's command broke into my thoughts. "Company — attention! To report to the lieutenant — eyes right!"

"*Heil*, comrades!"

"*Heil*, Lieutenant!"

"At ease!"

The lieutenant impressed me from the first. I guessed him to be about twenty-two or twenty-three years old. On his breast glittered the German Golden Cross, the degree just below the Knight's Cross.

"My name is Vogt. I am now your senior officer. Whether we get on well together depends primarily on you. I hope you are not more stupid than the recruits whom I have already trained. I dislike long speeches; deeds count for more, men. And for a soldier, honor is to be valued above all else." He shook hands with the corps leader, then gave the command, "Forward! — route step — march!"

An unfamiliar picture presented itself as we left the school yard. The corps leader lead us through the gate to the street. A truck was parked at the curb. Its canvas top was up, and a double-barreled machine gun, pointing up, was mounted above the driver's cab.

Two corporals came to attention and one reported, "No unusual occurrence, Lieutenant."

"Get in!" ordered the latter. That went for both the corporals and us. One corporal climbed over the tail gate with us, the other got into the cab with Lieutenant Vogt.

We made ourselves as comfortable as we could, while our corporal climbed up on the machine gun. "What a bunch of greenhorns!" I heard him mutter.

"By greenhorns perhaps you mean us?" Bubi demanded.

The corporal looked at him contemptuously. "I'll give you three guesses, kid."

Before Bubi had time to explode, the truck started with a jerk which threw us all together in a heap. We had to sort ourselves out and then hang on tight. The street was bumpy, and the driver was really stepping on the gas.

"That guy goes like a singed sow," grumbled the Bull.

"Listen to him!" grunted the corporal. "He isn't dry behind the ears yet, and he talks like an old hand." Karl Korner grinned. He thought the corporal was complimenting him.

"Where are we going?" I asked. The corporal looked down at me and growled, "I'll give you some good advice, laddie. The stupidest thing a soldier can do is ask too many silly questions. Keep your eyes open and you can see for yourself."

Not a very friendly companion! He had scorned us, so we ignored him.

By now we were all aware that the truck was leaving the city. Long Bayer struck up a song:

> *We want to march today*
> *In a new and different way . . .*

I joined loudly in the silly refrain —

*O-o-o-o you lovely western wood, Eucalyptus bom
bom!*
The wind in the treetops moans,
The cold could freeze your bones,
But the tiniest sunny ray
Makes our young hearts gay.

Our last sight of the city was of the two towers
of the famous old Gothic church as we drove south
into the forest.

"They're sending us to chop wood," Barbarossa
joked, but Schmidt whispered to me, "The forest is
a good place to be; they can't see us from the
air."

"Do you want to be a soldier or are you just
planning to go into hiding?" I asked angrily.
Schmidt hung his head and was silent.

No one was to be seen on either side of the road.
Schroeder started to speak. "Corporal —" He
didn't get any further. "Shut up, you jerk,"
grunted the corporal, and Schroeder also hung his
head. I didn't want to give the corporal another
chance to brush me off, but I was too annoyed to
keep still. Even if he did have two stripes on
his sleeve, he didn't have to treat us like dirt.

2 3

"Whether we're dopes remains to be seen!" I yelled.

Bubi backed me up. He pointed to Schneider. "Have you ever before seen a sixteen-year-old dope with the Military Cross of Merit, Corporal?"

"And what about your medals — you left them at home, no doubt?" sneered Bayer. Even Thumser joined in. "When I am a doctor, I'll operate on you with great pleasure, Corporal, free of charge!"

"Probably without anesthetic," the Bull said; so softly, however, that the fellow on the gun could not hear him. This was going pretty far; a soldier with two stripes is after all a person to be respected. Strangely enough, the corporal did not get angry. He merely looked at Schneider's medal and growled, "You kids don't know what you're letting yourselves in for."

"Will you be so kind as to explain what we are letting ourselves in for?" Walter Müller asked. The ever-courteous Walter! "Will you be so kind —" was one of his typical formalities.

"Some of you have enlisted voluntarily, right?"

"Right!" echoed Manfred Huber. "Any objections?"

"We would be drafted anyway," Gerngross added.

"Our battery can do without assistant gunners!" the corporal shouted.

"So what?" Bubi retorted.

The corporal looked disgusted. "Tell me now, are you really so stupid or are you just conceited?"

"We'll be glad to learn," Walter said.

"I'm thirty-four years old, with a wife and four children at home."

"So what?" from Bubi again.

The corporal gestured as if to push something away. "Oh, to hell with it!" He glared at us. "It doesn't matter whether you hear it from me or from somebody else. All I hope is that there isn't a dirty informer here."

"We didn't squeal on each other in school," Schneider said, entering the conversation for the first time. With a sidelong glance at Schroeder he continued, "Isn't that true, Opera Singer?"

Schroeder pretended not to hear him.

Schneider nodded to the corporal, who looked at each of us for reassurance, then shrugged.

"Okay, you heroes. We are stationed in an antiaircraft emplacement about seven kilometers from the city limits. There is an antiaircraft circle with a radius up to ten kilometers drawn around the city. Sure, you lived through a couple of air raids — in a shelter. The antiaircraft fighters who man the guns around the railroad stations or the munitions factories are the ones who get the worst of it. They can't crawl into hiding when the bombs come down like hail. It's a damned unequal fight between a couple of gun batteries and hundreds of four-engined bombers! I won't beat around the bush any longer. As soon as you are trained to take over the gun emplacements, the permanent staff and us regular soldiers can be transferred to the center of the city or to the Front in the west, east, or south. There the guns are used for ground fighting as well as antiaircraft, especially against armored tanks. The casualties are high.

"Perhaps you can understand now why we don't welcome you with open arms. Seven kilometers from the city we have been fairly safe. After years in the service we have had a snootful. Nobody wants to bite the dust. Then you greenhorns come along, release us for other "missions," as they are so beautifully called, and land us in the soup. That's what happens. And if any of you want to squeal on me to the Old Man, go ahead! Then Corporal Maier number two will be reduced in rank and thrown into the guardhouse. It all makes me sick!"

The ride was over. The driver jammed on the brake so suddenly that we were all thrown against one another again. The voice of the lieutenant drowned out our protests. "Dismount!" We jumped off the truck and formed ranks in a clearing in the pine forest. I knew the place well because I had often roamed through it with my father. An unused canal ran close by. Well under the trees three trucks and two jeeps were parked.

The driver put the truck under cover. Maier dismantled the machine gun, and Lieutenant Vogt ordered, "Come with me!" The clearing, out of which only a poor wagon road led, was merely a parking place. We marched in route step into the woods.

"Hey, you guys!" Long Bayer was excited. "That's an 8.8!" The first gun of "our" battery was mounted between trees which had been lopped off sufficiently to give it a long firing range. The barrel was pointed upward. To prevent the gun from being spotted by planes, a camouflage net was thrown over it. We halted at the lieutenant's command. "Have a look at the toy," he joked.

A soldier with steel helmet, rifle and binoculars came out from the trees and stood at attention before the lieutenant. "Private Grimm on guard. Nothing unusual." At the lieutenant's command he went back to his post.

I had eyes only for the gun. An 8.8! No ordinary two-centimeter gun, but a heavy piece. That was the surprise.

The lieutenant gave us time to examine the 8.8. He offered some explanations, but he apparently thought that he was talking to technicians. All I got out of it was that in this part of the forest a big battery, consisting of three 8.8 batteries, was hidden. Each battery had four guns. Then half underground there was a bomb-proof concrete shelter with three antiaircraft command sets, and in another place two radar sets had been constructed, to search the skies for enemy planes.

The lieutenant told us that he was in command of the second battery, to which this gun belonged. Then he said something about a field of traverse of twice 360 degrees and of a veined transmission cable which conveyed the firing data consecutively from the fire control. We tried to look interested but succeeded only in looking stupid; so the lieutenant gave up, laughing.

"All Greek to you? Never mind, you'll soon catch on. There is a time for everything, and now time presses, gentlemen. But perhaps you will be surprised to learn that this gun here has a remarkable history. Do you see the seven white rings on the barrel?"

We saw them.

"Each ring represents an enemy plane shot down — all American four-engined bombers."

I poked Thumser. "Man, Otto, isn't that something!"

"May I ask you, lieutenant, how much an 8.8 shell weighs?" This of course was Schroeder.

"Nineteen pounds. But we've talked enough. Let's go."

"My little brother weighs nineteen pounds," Bubi murmured.

"Do you weigh more?" Korner teased him.

"Don't be foolish; you can't make that sort of comparison," Gerngross said.

"Watch out!" warned the lieutenant. We had to be careful about where we walked since there were trenches all around running at right and acute angles; this arrangement, I realized, afforded the best protection. We stumbled into another man-made clearing where there were two guns. The lieutenant waved away the report from the guard. At some distance beyond was a massive concrete block which the lieutenant said was the command shelter. There all the information was collected, and during an attack the necessary orders were given to the batteries. "You realize that the tele-phone, radio and control center must be in a bomb-proof place. Unfortunately there is not much room in the shelter; so if in the next few days an air-raid alarm should be given, you must dive into the trenches. More shelters will be built shortly. The commander of our emplacement is First Lieu-tenant Vollmer."

Some soldiers appeared, saluted the lieutenant, stared at us, and went away. Here and there some of them put their heads together and talked in low voices after the lieutenant had gone. Most of them were older men, and they seemed as glum as Corporal Maier number two.

Then we came to the barracks: four long wooden buildings in a clearing, carefully camouflaged. Out of three on the left, curious faces stared at us. Here, too, there were sullen looks. Corporal Maier was right; the "old comrades" had no intention of welcoming us with open arms.

Lieutenant Vogt led us to the barracks which was at the furthest right. The door flew open and a corporal who looked about thirty years old came out and saluted with his left hand. When I looked more closely at his stiff right arm, I saw that it was artificial. What impressed me most were the decorations he wore: the Iron Cross, Second Class, the Iron Cross, First Class, and a silver wound pin.

"Here they are, Haberzettel," the lieutenant said.

The corporal's answer was a growl. He sounded far from enthusiastic and certainly not friendly.

"Install these people, Haberzettel," the lieutenant ordered.

"Certainly, Lieutenant." Then to us, "Come along."

✠ 3 ✠

Getting Acquainted
with Our Quarters

OUR BARRACKS had two rooms. One served as both
living room and dormitory, with twelve upper and
lower bunks for us and a single bed for Corporal
Haberzettel, seven lockers, a long table, thirteen
chairs, and an iron stove. On the windowless wall
hung a picture of the Führer. A partition with a
door in it separated this room from the other, into
which the corporal took us next.

"Here you will be given technical instruction,
explanation of the service regulations, use of guns,
identification of planes by their markings, and so
forth and so on."

It looked like a schoolroom. Everything was
there: two rows of benches, blackboard, the instructor's desk and chair. Only the pictures were of
a military nature. They showed the 8.8 in diagonal

and transverse sections, the separate parts, as well as a drawing indicating the trajectory of the missile.

Haberzettel ordered us back into the living room. "You will be kept together," he informed us, "and I am your group leader. We belong to the battery of Lieutenant Vogt. If you have a good conduct record and aren't too stupid, you may go home over the weekend, three of you at a time. So each of you will see your mother once a month. Anyone who thinks he has something to complain of comes to me first. That clear?"

"Yes, Corporal!"

He became a shade friendlier. "So you can grumble if you like, a little anyway. My name's Haberzettel. And yours?"

"Bayer."

"Antiaircraft Assistant Gunner Bayer," Haberzettel reminded him. "How old?"

"Sixteen and three-quarters, Corporal."

"Nonsense, Bayer, we don't count fractions." He pointed to the next.

"Gunner Braun, Corporal, sixteen."

"Gunner Schneider, Corporal, sixteen."

"Military Cross of Merit?"

"Yes, Corporal."

"For what?"

"I dragged a boy out of a burning house after a bombing attack."

"Why you? Were there no adults near?"

"Yes, Corporal, but the house was about to collapse. They said it was too dangerous to go near it."

"Hm!" The corporal sounded less stern. "Go on."

"Gunner Briel, Corporal, sixteen."

Gunner Schroeder, Gunner Schmidt, Gunner Korner, Gunner Huber, Gunner Thumser, Gunner Müller, Gunner Hauschild, Gunner Gerngross. Each sixteen.

What a memory Haberzettel had! After the roll call, he pointed to each one of us and gave the right name. Only when he came to Hauschild did he have to think for a second.

"Put away your gear." We stowed the little bundles we had brought from home in the lockers. Then we went with him to get our outfits. It had become very lively outside because a big group of the regular army had arrived. We ran the gauntlet through a line of sullen, curious, but friendly soldiers. Two of them wore the Iron Cross, Second Class and the silver wound pin, like Haberzettel.

"Have you opened a kindergarten, Hans?" one of them jeered.

Haberzettel scowled at him. "Go to blazes! I'm mad enough without your nonsense!"

The commissary barracks lay a little farther into the forest. Here we met Maier number one, the quartermaster, a corporal like our Maier but much jollier. He spoke to our corporal with a distinct Austrian accent. "Well, well, and what have you here? All your own?"

Haberzettel swore roundly, and Maier number one became businesslike. He turned to the shelf behind him and handed out sheets, blankets, checked quilts, shirts, socks, underpants, declaring with each item, "It fits!" Back to our barracks through the crowd of regulars, we unloaded, then returned to Maier number one. He tossed to us boots, jackets, pants, coats, and steel helmets. When we went back to our barracks this time, some of the regulars had gone. We were no longer of much interest.

What a keen eye Maier number one had! When

we tried the things on we were amazed — almost nothing fitted. My helmet was too big and hung down over my eyes and ears, and my pants were too short. My two boots were of different sizes. The others were as badly off as I. "You can't do any exchanging at the commissary, so swap with one another," Haberzettel advised. We did this until finally we all looked somewhat human. I was proud; I was wearing a uniform — a real one. I was a soldier!

"Make your beds." The corporal did not allow slipshod appearances. Straw mattress, sheets, and blankets must be fixed so that the corners formed perfect right angles. Then we had an hour free before going to the classroom.

"Want to play chess, Gabriel?" Alfred Schmidt asked. "I brought my set with me."

"You have a nerve!" I retorted. "I want to go and look the place over."

"I'll come with you," Gerngross offered. When we went out, a couple of regulars who had waited outside took us into their quarters. They probably wanted to get to know us better. Two younger gunners, privates, came over to us. We thought that we should salute, for whoever wore a chevron ranked above us, but they waved that aside. They asked where we came from, and when I said that most of us were volunteers, one of them clapped me on the shoulder. "The Führer should be proud of such boys. I enlisted, too; I really wanted to go to the Front, but I got stuck in this dull place where nothing ever happens. Now that you are here, some of us can be released for combat missions. I'll be with the first detachment that leaves — at last!" He shook my hand. "I'm Wittmann from Bremen."

We gave our names and were told that the other soldier, Heinrich Heller, came from Breslau. Both were former Hitler Youth leaders, impatient to get away, sure of being able to take care of themselves. I felt relieved. There were other types besides Maier number two in the place.

"Corporal Haberzettel acts like a grouch, but he isn't one at all, and Lieutenant Vogt is a superb officer. You'll learn a great deal from them both, though at the beginning you won't find it easy."

"We have had premilitary training," I protested.

"In the Hitler Youth," Gerngross added.

Wittmann laughed. "But you didn't get gunnery training or much of ground defense."

"You're here in the antiaircraft emplacement, not with the infantry," Heller reminded us.

"We should like to look around," I suggested. They both agreed to guide us. We saw that the four guns of the battery, placed four or five meters apart, made a square. The three batteries formed a triangle in the center of which the command shelter stood. At some distance from the guns were the radar equipment and searchlights, and Wittmann showed us a new type of sound locator near the shelter. Everywhere guards were posted with guns slung over their shoulders. Our barracks and that of the officers were outside the area of the gun sites.

"An attack by an enemy plane on an antiaircraft emplacement is directed first against the guns," Wittmann explained. "That's why the living quarters are at a safe distance."

"Which doesn't mean," Heller chimed in, "that you may remain in the barracks when the alarm sounds. Those who are not manning the guns or other apparatus have to go into the trenches."

Wittmann laughed. "There you will be as safe

38

as in Abraham's bosom — unless you get hit on the head with a bomb!"

"You have a nerve," muttered Gerngross.

"On the contrary, kid, I have no nerves. We have to do without them. The Führer needs soldiers, not bundles of nerves."

"Anyway you don't have to do your own thinking," Heller went on; "your superior officers do it for you. When you are carrying out orders at lightning speed, you're hardly conscious of what's happening."

Gerngross wanted to protest; he started to speak, then thought better of it. We went back to our barracks. The privates had looked at the clock and explained that they must relieve the sentries at the radar location.

In our barracks we found our comrades and two older artillery men. They monopolized the conversation and boasted about their experiences in France before they were transferred here. Bayer, Schroeder, Barbarossa, the Bull, and Bubi listened open-mouthed. But Schmidt, Schneider, Huber, Thumser, and Müller perched on the bunks and were not listening. They were embarrassed; their faces were red. As Gerngross and I caught a few sentences about the "fighters in France" we, too, were ashamed, because the men were not speaking of battles but of "gallantries" with a certain kind of woman in a certain kind of place.

"Swine!" Gerngross spoke with disgust. The two men grinned, but Bubi jumped up. "Do you mean me?" he yelled, clenching his fists. Gerngross merely replied, unperturbed, "Whoever listens to filthy talk is just as swinish as the speaker."

I stood close to Gerngross and turned my sleeves back. In an instant two sides were drawn up. Only the two privates sat grinning. "Something new for a change, Schorsch," one of them commented, "a fight in the kindergarten."

Nothing came of it, however. The door flew open suddenly. "Attention!" bellowed Long Bayer. I pulled my sleeves down quickly and stiffened like the others. Corporal Haberzettel had come in. "Get out!" he ordered the visitors, then to us, "Stay at attention. You are about to have visitors."

Lieutenant Vogt came first. He made a sign to the corporal not to announce the visitors, looked quickly around, said, "Well, a great pleasure," saluted, and went over to the side. If we had not already come to attention, we would have done so at this point — without a command. For the visitors were Nero and Point-five, our Latin and math teachers!

We called Nero that because he "persecuted" us with his Latin classics. The math teacher owed his name to a phrase he constantly threw at us: "Think, gentlemen, think! I expect the answer in point-five." I was afraid of Nero; my knowledge of Latin was at best only average. I had no fear of Point-five since in math I was at the head of the class. In spite of this I liked math less than Latin; this had nothing to do with math and Latin — the reason was personal.

Point-five spoke of the Führer and the Thousand Year Empire* only when he couldn't help it, and what he said was distinctly lacking in enthusiasm. However, what he said was so skillfully phrased that it could not be held against him. The housemaster of our school had once called him "traitor," and he was remarkably well informed.

In this regard Nero was quite the opposite; he had been for some time a member of the Nazi

* A boast of Hitler that his "Third Empire" would outlast time.

41

party and various related groups, and he was besides a brilliant platform speaker. A true follower of the Führer! If only he weren't a Latin teacher. He appeared now in the uniform of a political leader; Point-five wore civilian clothes.

The lieutenant and corporal left at a signal from Nero. *"Heil* Hitler!" he cried, giving the Nazi salute, rigid arm lifted to shoulder level.

"Heil, sir." Our answer was not exactly enthusiastic; Schroeder drowned the rest of us out. Point-five merely nodded with no expression in his face.

"At ease!" Nero ordered, then "Sit!"

"Damn!" muttered Huber behind me. "That sounds just like school, and we are soldiers!"

Nero was very friendly; that was something new. As a rule he was stiff when speaking to inferiors. "Well, gunners, have you got settled?"

"Yes, sir," Schroeder brayed.

"The jerk!" Müller said under his breath.

Nero laughed. "Very good, excellent. I'm glad to hear it."

Point-five did not speak. He bit his underlip and seemed ill at ease. We perched on our stools and waited expectantly.

"I will not torment you," Nero continued. "The

purpose of our coming here can be expressed in a little motto: *Mens sana in corpore sano.* You can translate that easily, Huber?"

"A sound mind in a sound body."

"Good! Our superior officers guarantee the sound bodies; we, the sound minds. That's why we're here." He bowed slightly toward Point-five. "Dr. Winkler and I."

"That sounds as if they're going to stay," muttered Barbarossa but not softly enough.

Nero laughed again. "What's the matter, Braun? If you are worrying because of the stupid tricks you used to play on me, I can set your mind at rest. I don't hold them against you. Did you think I did?"

"No, sir, I — I . . ."

"Well, Braun?"

Gerngross came to his rescue. "Braun was surprised that you had another star on your collar, sir."

Nero nodded to Gerngross, then to Braun. "Yes, I was promoted by courtesy of the district leader. Now to the business at hand."

Braun gave a sigh of relief. Under the table he kicked Gerngross in the shins by way of reward.

Nero continued, "Dr. Winkler and I are exempt from military service, not because of our age, but because the Führer has required that the education of the young not be neglected even during the most bitter ordeal of the German people. When the war is over, Germans will be needed who are capable of healing the wounds inflicted by the war, and each according to his ability will open the way to a glorious future for people and country. You, my soldiers and students, will be grateful to us then that we are giving you the chance now to prepare for your future. I shall instruct you every day in Latin, German, and history. Dr. Winkler will give you another hour of mathematics and physics."

My mouth went dry. Latin and school math at a gun emplacement! If that wasn't a joke! I looked at Point-five. He showed nothing; not a muscle of his face twitched.

Books, notebooks, and whatever else he had requested for the schoolwork would arrive in a few days, Nero explained. The instruction would be arranged so that our military training would not suffer. If any of us needed advice or help, we would find Dr. Winkler and him in the officers' barracks.

Then Point-five spoke quietly, but I could see that he was disturbed. "After our headmaster reported for duty at the Front, Assistant Headmaster Dr. Ammon was appointed provisional headmaster." Dr. Ammon was Nero.

With a brief command, "Carry on!" Nero beckoned his colleague, and they left the barracks. We were so bewildered that Bayer called, "Attention!" after the two men had left.

Bubi was furious. "We're soldiers now, and we still haven't got rid of our teachers!"

"Attention!" This time it was the Bull who gave the warning, since he was the first to see the lieutenant and the corporal. We were ordered into the classroom and given our daily schedule: reveille at 6:00, exercises, 6:15; breakfast, 6:25 . . . everything was planned to the minute: duty, dinner, lessons, gun cleaning, room cleaning. The corporal lectured us about cleanliness in the barracks, air-raid conduct, and the need for silence.

Dinner was at 12:30, lentils and something Karl Korner called hash substitute. A half hour after eating we had to clean our quarters, giving the place a high polish with buckets, scrubbing brushes, and brooms. The corporal growled out his satisfaction; that was really something!

After that we received rifles, bayonets, cartridge pouches, spades, gas masks, and five rounds of ammunition for each soldier. Haberzettel watched vigilantly to be sure that the cartridges were put in the pouches in the proper way and the pouches then locked according to regulations. He evidently didn't wholly trust our premilitary training.

Maier number one, the quartermaster, grinned genially. "Shoot well!" Wittmann and Heller were waiting for us in front of the supply depot. "The apparatus is set up," Wittmann reported to the corporal, who then lined us up and, with the two privates, marched us through the woods to a nearby stone pit. This was the rifle range.

We aimed lying flat at a hundred meters' distance. Wittmann called out the shots, and Heller kept the record. Haberzettel watched us, at first distrustfully; then his face brightened more and more. We were no dopes. Only Schmidt, top student in class work, did badly. To begin with he missed, then shot a three, finally a five. Huber was in his element; he got a ten, twelve, eleven.

"Line up!" Haberzettel called out at the finish. "Tomorrow we can send you on guard duty." We marched back to the barracks, but anyone who thought we'd be free now was in for a disappointment.

"Instruction," the corporal announced, "then gun cleaning."

First he taught us about the 8.8, largely what we had already learned from Lieutenant Vogt. At the end we learned from a model to recognize the mechanical parts of the machine gun. That was the first practical manual exercise. The time was all too short.

Cleaning the guns was nothing new to us although the corporal was more strict in his inspection than our leader in the Hitler Youth. When he held the open rifles up to the light, he couldn't find a speck of dust in the barrel. Roll call ended the duty, and Lieutenant Vogt, "in celebration of the day" as he said, conducted it himself. He had no complaints to make, and we went to supper, which consisted of bread, margarine, cheese, and tea.

✠ 4 ✠

October 3, 1944

SIX O'CLOCK REVEILLE, exercises in front of the barracks, breakfast, and so on, according to the schedule. Lieutenant Vogt presented us to the Old Man, the commander of the whole battery. First Lieutenant Vollmer was barely twenty-six years old, yet he had a full row of medals, among them two Rumanian Orders. A prime daredevil, he had a series of field actions against armored tanks behind him, and had joined our detachment only because he was no longer able to serve at the Front. He had been wounded four times, and walked with a cane. What he had to say was not particularly remarkable, but he found the right note for us.

"As antiaircraft gunners you are soldiers; as soldiers you have to do your duty and obey every order blindly, otherwise — go to the devil. Prove that you are not babies! Thank you."

Lieutenant Vogt then divided us into two groups of six. The first, to which I belonged, was to learn defense tactics under Haberzettel. The second Vogt led to shooting practice. After an hour we were to exchange places.

Haberzettel was merciless. Again and again he shouted, "Take full cover!" and we had to throw ourselves into the nearest hollow or get behind the nearest tree or mound. For a change we dived into the trenches and pressed our faces against the earth. He made us get a move on; when an air attack really came, he declared, we'd know why we had to have such stiff training.

And what a vocabulary! "Full cover. Pull in your rump, Schroeder, or do you want it to be shaved off by a mine?" He didn't miss a thing. When Huber's helmet slid to the back of his neck and he raised his arms to put it straight, Haberzettel blasted him. "What's the matter? Have you got Saint Vitus's dance? The jerk does gym exercises when he's supposed to be under cover! Do you want to draw the attention of the whole English air force to us? — Always in the soup, Gerngross! When it's heavy firing, you don't look for a dry place first! — Put your teeth into it, Bayer! What a dope! By the time you get into position, the war will be over. That goes for you too, Briel. Speed is half the battle. Get your grandmother to teach you how to run. When I give the command to march, I don't want to see anything but bootheels and leveled bayonets."

We were in a devil of a sweat, although we had been accustomed to some of this in the Hitler Youth. But now I knew the difference between premilitary training and the real thing. Not one of us slacked off, and the corporal grudgingly acknowledged it. "Okay, not bad for a start."

A five-minute pause, then to the guns. Lieutenant Vogt also forced the pace. Those who had been doing the gun loading showed us the knack. Of course we used practice grenades. The 8.8 swung into action. The half-automatic action of the gun allowed for rapid firing, and if the loader wasn't on hand with the next round, the gun pointer would storm, and the gunner explode.

The officers did not seem to know the meaning of patience. They believed that what they had had plenty of time to learn we must grasp in the flick of a hand. "Each of you must master the most important manipulations of the gun," Vogt insisted. "In an emergency you must be ready to replace each other."

A five-minute recess, then back to the classroom where Vogt told us what he expected of each of us individually. Every evening, from eight to ten, three of us would have sentry duty. The later hours of the night watch would be taken over at first by the regular soldiers. We would be taught how we must act on watch: eyes and ears open; on the slightest suspicion challenge once, then fire!

Special duties were assigned as follows: Gerngross and Hauschild, telephone operators; Thumser and Huber at the range finder; Müller and Schneider, guards at the sound locator; Schroeder, Braun, and Schmidt, guards at the searchlights. Bayer, Korner, and I would be trained as gun loaders. The others looked enviously at us, and we felt like big shots. But the Lieutenant assured them that their service was just as important as ours; besides, all would be instructed in the 8.8.

We were next taught to recognize enemy planes through diagrams. Much of this we already knew.

Our city had previously suffered several air attacks, and the newspapers were continually publishing illustrations of enemy bombers. But this instruction we were receiving now was more exact: American pursuit plane P-14 Thunderbolt, destroyer and pursuit bomber P-38 Lightning, medium combat plane B-26 Marauder, heavy four-engined bomber B-17 Fortress and B-29 Superfortress; then the English and Russian planes.

"The Russians are of less importance for us," the lieutenant said, "because they are not likely to come near us after Bavaria. But heaven help any of you who confuse a Spitfire with a Thunderbolt!"

In the afternoon we had our first Latin lesson with Nero: Ovid! And he was the Roman writer for whom I cared least. Although Nero had arranged to have a book for everyone, I was miles away from Ovid, my thoughts dwelling on the 8.8.

"Briel!" Nero's voice dragged me back to the lesson. I jumped up and clicked my heels. Nero loved military gestures. "Were you asleep, Briel?"

"No, sir."

"Very good, Briel. Then you can certainly tell me what Ovid means when he writes —"

At the last second I was saved by — the bombs! A heavy explosion ripped the words from Nero's mouth, the floor and the walls of the barracks shook, the windows rattled. No commands were necessary. We took complete cover by disappearing under the benches. I lay on the floor, protecting my head with my hands and holding my breath. No one spoke; one could have heard the proverbial pin fall. Nothing more happened; no second detonation followed, and all was quiet in the camp.

No alarm!

A head came up near mine — Long Bayer's. He had pulled himself together first. *Mens sana in corpore sano.* He was grinning. "I think I am all in one piece; my corpus is intact, and I can even think."

"Bombs!" I said softly.

Bayer tapped me lightly on the forehead. "Very clever, Gabriel! They weren't Easter eggs, that's for sure."

"But there wasn't any plane! We would have heard the droning!"

Bayer shrugged. "I'm no clairvoyant." We crawled out even though Nero hadn't said a word. When I pushed my head above the desk, I saw his face; it was the color of chalk. He leaned on the table, clutching Ovid with both hands. Finally he spoke, even his voice trembling. "Why was no alarm given?"

There was a knock on the door, and Point-five stepped in, looking much as always. "Excuse me," he said to Nero, "Lieutenant Vogt held me up; that's why I'm so late. However, I see that the gunners are on the alert."

"What happened?" Nero demanded.

"First Lieutenant Vollmer warned me ten minutes ago that bombs would be exploded about four kilometers from the camp. English and American dud bombs that had to be rendered harmless. Army engineers took care of the exploding. The Staff asked me to inform the gunners; however, Herr Vogt asked me to wait until after the detonation."

"And — why, may I ask?" Nero was still gasping.

Lieutenant Vogt himself gave the answer, appearing at that moment. "Very good, nobody fainted!"

"I wish an explanation, Lieutenant!" Nero burst out. He was no longer pale, but red and shaking with anger.

"Here it comes," Korner whispered. "Watch, this is going to be a real fight!"

Vogt, however, was not annoyed at Nero's challenge. "I wanted to find out how my gunners behaved when the explosion was unexpected." He turned to us. "Did you take full cover?"

"Certainly, Lieutenant." The tension eased. We were proud of ourselves, and besides, he had said "*my* gunners!"

"Insolence!" Nero hissed.

"I'm sorry I had to frighten you, sir," Vogt said, quietly.

Nero, who had been panting with rage, got hold of himself. "You have disturbed my Latin class, Lieutenant."

"Not intentionally, Doctor, I wanted only to put the gunners to the test." He saluted and left. Nero gripped his Ovid under his arm and turned to Point-five. "Please take over the class, Doctor."

As the math teacher went to the desk, Nero beckoned to the opera singer. "Come with me, Schroeder."

"Certainly, Assistant Headmaster." Nero did not rebuke him for using the old title, and the two left.

"Dangerous situation!" Bayer was grinning. "We'll squeeze it out of the opera singer when he comes back."

Dr. Winkler tapped on the desk. "Quiet, please!" But Bayer was in his element. "Nero was scared stiff," he crowed.

"Shut up!" I growled at him. But he was irrepressible. "At home he has a bomb-proof cellar, but here —"

Under the bench I kicked him in the shins, and that silenced him.

Point-five smiled. "We shall try to put mathematics at the service of the military. As you know, a shell trajectory never takes a straight course. That is especially true when a more distant target comes under fire. The curvature of the line of flight can be calculated. I think that, as gunners, you will find such calculations interesting."

We were absorbed by the lesson. Schroeder

came back toward the end of the period. He was silent and had a mysterious air. "This evening he'll be thrashed until he sings," declared the Bull.

In the late afternoon we marched with the corporal, Wittmann and Heller to the stone pit for machine gun practice. We tried single shots, then sustained fire. Manfred Huber was the star performer again, but I was satisfied with my shots, which were not too wide of the mark.

After supper the noncommissioned officers of our battery were summoned to receive orders in the shelter. We gunners were alone in our barracks.

"All set?" Karl Korner, the Bull, inquired.

Long Bayer spit on his hands. "Ready!"

"Let's go!" Bubi said gleefully.

The three walked slowly toward Schroeder, cut off his escape through the door, and dragged him into the corner. "What did Nero want you for?" Bayer demanded.

Bubi clenched his fists. "Spit it out!"

Schroeder turned pale. "Leave me alone!" he gasped. "It was nothing special — just a personal matter."

"We're a big family," Huber was grinning,

"and in a family there are no secrets. Your brothers are curious, little Schroeder!"

"I — I'll tell you!" Schroeder burst out. He shouldn't have said that. Bayer picked him up by his jacket and swung him back and forth. "Give!"

Schroeder didn't try to defend himself. He put his hands over his face and whimpered. Korner and Bubi grabbed him and threw him from one to the other. Suddenly Barbarossa stuck out his leg and tripped him. Hauschild, Braun, and Huber threw themselves on top of him.

"Disgusting!" muttered Gerngross.

Schneider, Schmidt, Müller, and Thumser stood aside like Gerngross. Then I saw red. Schroeder had been punched in the nose, and he was crying. Although I had never been able to stand him, I threw myself between him and his persecutors. "Cut it out, you big bullies!" I yanked Bubi off, punched the Bull, and grabbed Barbarossa by the collar. Schneider rushed to my side, then Thumser, Müller, and Schmidt. Only Gerngross stayed out of the fight. He shook his head. "So that's what they call comradeship!"

In no time the wildest brawl was under way. No one thought any more about Schroeder. We punched each other, chairs were flung around, the table tipped over. Korner was panting like a bull, Bayer was cursing, and Bubi shrieking with rage. The barracks shook. It was like a high-voltage explosion.

"Stop!" It was a knife-sharp command. We let go of each other and took deep, gasping breaths. Private Wittmann stood in the door. "Have you gone crazy? Your racket could be heard three kilometers away! What's the matter?"

We stood with our heads hanging. I noticed that Schroeder had quietly slipped out of the room.

"I want to know what's the matter!" Wittmann thundered.

Bayer stepped forward. "Nothing special, Private Wittmann. We — we just couldn't agree on how best to express the meaning of comradeship."

Wittmann did not inquire further. "Two buttons are missing from your jacket, Gunner," he said to Bayer. And to Korner, "There's a spot of blood on your left sleeve." Then to all of us, "You don't look like soldiers but like hoodlums after a tavern brawl. Tidy yourselves up! And look at the room! In twenty minutes this place has got to be in apple-pie order. Get going!" He stayed to watch while we worked like mad, cleaning, polishing, repairing all at once. Gerngross helped those who couldn't manage alone.

"What you have done is quite different from the ordinary stupid tricks of kids," Wittmann rebuked us sharply. "You know that you are supposed to be releasing trained soldiers for duty at the Front. Instead of which you break one another's skulls. If I had not come along and heard the row, some of you would be ready for the hospital. That would be a fine way to serve the Führer! It comes dangerously close to undermining the war effort, sirs! Apparently you have not been disciplined enough. I'll tell you this: if I should be kept from going to the Front on account of you, you won't live to see it!"

We got through the work before the time limit Wittmann had set. He lined us up and inspected each one. "You're lucky," he growled, "I might have had to report you."

As if it had been prearranged, Corporal Haberzettel came back at that precise moment.

"Attention!" Wittmann commanded, then made his report: "Private Wittmann giving special instruction in comradeship. Nothing particular to report."

Haberzettel nodded to Wittmann. "Not a bad idea; it will keep these kids from getting off on the wrong track. At ease! Dismissed!"

"Private Wittmann asks leave to go."

"All right, Wittmann, good night."

"Good night, Corporal. Good night, Gunners."

"Good night, Private Wittmann!" Bubi spoke the loudest. Long Bayer was very subdued, and Korner only muttered the words.

"Where is Schroeder?" the corporal asked.

"He — he stepped out, Corporal," Bubi stammered.

A few minutes later Schroeder returned. We stared. What would happen now?

"Man alive, what a sight you are!" Haberzettel exclaimed. The boy's nose had stopped bleeding, but his face was smeared with blood. A button was missing from his jacket, and the poor chap looked thoroughly beaten up.

He tried to pull himself together. "I — I went out, Corporal, and then — then I stumbled and fell."

"What a fine soldier you are! I give you ten minutes to get into shape. Understand?"

"Yes, Corporal."

"I'd never have believed he wouldn't squeal on us," Müller whispered to me.

"I'll help you, Schroeder," I offered. He gave me a look that I couldn't fathom.

At eight o'clock that evening I stood watch with Bayer and Thumser. Corporal Haberzettel assigned us the sections we were to patrol, each on his own. We separated, and I began my round. It was bitingly cold. I pulled up the collar of my coat, listened for sounds in the woods, and looked at the empty sky. There was no deep droning in the distance to betray the approach of enemy bombers. It would probably be a quiet night.

Suddenly I quivered. There were steps in the darkness. I tore the gun from my shoulder and released the safety catch. My voice sounded strange as I shouted the first word of the password: "Halt! Elector!" If it was one of us he would know the second word.

"August!" came the reply. Right. In a moment Schroeder stood beside me. "You don't have guard duty; what do you want?"

"Don't speak so loudly, Briel; I sneaked out."

"Why? Are they still tormenting you?"

"No, but you were the first to come to my aid. I saw that all right."

"So what? Four against one is a rotten trick."

"And then you helped me to get cleaned up."

"In ten minutes you couldn't possibly have done it alone. So just forget it."

"No, Briel. Before this I had hardly any friends, and you —"

I interrupted him. "Who said I'm your friend?"

Schroeder gulped. "You know, Briel, here everything is different from at home and in school, and I've felt very alone. Then you came to help me —"

"We've been over that, Schroeder!"

"I wish you'd be my friend, Briel."

"That's something that has to come of itself, Schroeder."

"It's a request, Briel, and I promise that you can trust me. If I tell you — only you — what Nero wanted me for —"

"Hm!"

"You'll keep it to yourself?"

"I am not forcing you to tell me."

"Good, I'll trust you anyway," Schroeder said with relief.

I was excited, but I didn't want him to see it, because I didn't want him to think he could twist me around so quickly. It was only because I had wanted to see fair play that I had helped him out, not from any friendly feeling.

"Nero is not only a Latin teacher but a high official in the party, Briel."

"What surprising information," I sneered.

Schroeder gave no sign of being offended but begged, "Do listen to me, Briel!"

"That's what I've been doing all this time!"

"Nero took me into the officers' barracks. Each of them has his own room. He said he knew that my father was an ardent National Socialist and knew also that I would do anything I could for the Führer and the party."

"We all intend to do that." I was angry that Nero had given the opera singer the confidence he should have given me. Was it perhaps that Schroeder was better in Latin than I, and Nero thought Ovid was as important as a political attitude? Nonsense! There must be something else behind it. Now I was nearly bursting with curiosity. "Go on, Schroeder."

"Nero said that not everyone was so loyal, and that is why he had come to the antiaircraft emplacement — to find out whether the Hitler Youth were in the right hands."

"He meant us gunners," I interrupted.

"Right. He said that the insignia on a uniform does not mean that the wearer is a National Socialist whom one could trust, and that the party badge on the lapel gives no reason for confidence. There are actually party members who have serious doubts of the final victory."

"Then they're dopes or blackguards!"

"Nero said something like that, too."

The suspense was unbearable. "Well, what else," I prompted him. "Did he hint at anyone in particular in the camp?"

"Not directly."

Then I lost patience. "Come on, what did he say?" Schroeder was so near that I could make out his face in the darkness.

"Nero didn't make me promise to keep silent. He only threatened that it would be bad for me if our conversation came to the wrong ears. But you're all right, I know."

"Make it snappy," I growled. "I'm on guard duty. If someone comes to check and sees us together, there'll be trouble."

"I am supposed to listen and notice who tells jokes about the Führer, Goebbels, Goering, Himmler, and the other high-ranking officials, and who spreads enemy propaganda or otherwise undermines the fighting spirit. Then I am to report to him. And —"

"And?" I encouraged him as he paused.

He said nothing until I seized him by the collar. "I'll tell, really!" He lowered his voice to a barely audible whisper. "I am to observe closely whether — Lieutenant Vogt and Point-five let fall any remarks which — in this sense could be considered subversive."

I couldn't believe I had heard correctly. "Vogt is an officer, Schroeder!"

"Not so loud, Briel! That's what Nero meant by the insignia on the uniform. The conspiracy of July twentieth was planned by officers."

"Vogt is quite different!"

"We hardly know him," Schroeder objected.

"And Point-five is a party member!"

"Only in name, Briel."

"Did Nero say that?"

Schroeder evaded my question, but continued, "We all know it. He appeared at party meetings only when he couldn't get out of it, and if you compare him with Nero, the difference between them is obvious."

I didn't know what to think. Of course I believed that those who cast doubts on the party were villains and traitors — but Lieutenant Vogt? Nor did Point-five fall into this category if I judged correctly. Moreover, I found Nero's conduct unworthy of an officer. Why did he single out Lieutenant Vogt? Was he trying to get revenge for that incident in the Latin class? Out of the question! That would be petty, no — worse than that!

"You'll keep this to yourself, Briel," Schroeder whispered, "and now we have something we share — we two!"

"Stop your noise, Schroeder, someone is coming!"

We could clearly hear footsteps. "Keep it to yourself, Briel!" and Schroeder hurried away to the barracks.

I brought my gun into position. "Halt! Elector!"

"Go to blazes, Gabriel!" It was Long Bayer. What eyes he must have. He had recognized me and let his gun hang down as he came to my position in making his round.

"Who were you talking with, Gabriel?"

"You've got a bee in your bonnet."

"Don't try to fool me!"

"Oh, knock it off!" I growled.

"For a sentry you're terribly nervous, little Briel," he said in a mocking tone.

I swore at him, and we separated. I was breathing heavily as he disappeared in the darkness.

✠ 5 ✠

The Night of October 3, 1944

AFTER BEING RELIEVED of sentry duty, I hit the
sack, but before I went to sleep, I wanted to think
about Schroeder, Lieutenant Vogt, Point-five, and
Nero. About Nero especially. The picture I had
drawn of him was false. But, I did not get far.
Weariness overcame me; I slept. . . .

A piercing whistle roused me. The shrillness of
the alarm would wake the dead. Corporal Haberzettel could produce a remarkable volume of
sound. A dim light shone in the room.

"Air-raid alarm!" the corporal roared. "Battle
uniforms and full kit!" Everyone was now awake.
We hurried into our clothes, got tangled in them,
and finally straightened out. Haberzettel acted as
if this were an ordinary exercise. He checked our
drill formation as we fell into line in front of the
barracks.

Wild activity went on in the emplacement. The effect was weird because there was so little noise. Here and there a half-loud command was given, a light flashed briefly and went out. The regulars knew what they had to do. I had a strange feeling in my stomach. It was all very different from what I had imagined. None of us was allowed to man the guns. They didn't trust us yet.

"Keep quiet and listen for my commands," Haberzettel ordered. At that moment the wind carried the screaming of the sirens over from the city. Otherwise there was nothing to hear or see. Point-five appeared, nodded to the corporal and stood on the left flank near Gerngross as if he belonged to us.

The stillness was suddenly broken. First faintly, then always more distinctly came the barking of the discharges from the heavy antiaircraft guns. The fire was directed toward the northwest; so the bombers must be coming from that direction. They would first be attacked by the batteries bordering on the city, then by the guns placed in the center of the city in steplike formation.

No one except Haberzettel and Point-five bothered about us. Once I heard Lieutenant Vogt giving commands at the guns. Now came the heavy droning sound. We all recognized it — American four-engined bombers. The antiaircraft guns continued firing, even more furiously. Between the detonations of the 8.8 shells the machine guns clattered with a hard, dry sound: two-centimeter antiaircraft guns and those of our pursuit planes and of the enemy fighter escorts. There were constant flashes in the northwest. Searchlights swept the sky.

Then all hell broke loose. Thunderclaps shook the earth, which became an inferno. The bombers had reached the city and opened their shafts. Air mines, high explosives and fire bombs rained down. The screaming of the bombs and the crashing of their targets became one noise.

Sharp commands at the guns!

"Take full cover!" Haberzettel shouted. "Into the trenches and heads down!" We flung ourselves into the trenches and pressed close to the ground. Searchlight beams pierced the sky and planes droned over the city. On their return flight they flew over our emplacement.

Lieutenant Vogt's commands were sharp but betrayed no excitement. Fuse setting, direction.

. . . The droning of the bombers was deafening.

"Battery two — open fire!" Vogt shouted. The discharge made the ground tremble. Then a bomb dived down, struck near us in the woods, making a hellish noise.

Twice — three times — four times! Earth spurted up, trees were shattered, fragments of rock, split trunks, and branches whirled around and crashed down in great masses in front of us. Near the second gun someone screamed. The noise of the planes grew louder; the guns of our battery fired steadily; commands rang out.

I raised my head cautiously but ducked down again as a rock struck and sprayed dirt in my face. Now I was shaking with fear. Although it was too dark to see anything, I closed my eyes. This was different from an air-raid shelter — damnably different! I lay under the open sky, and only blind chance could protect me. No ceiling of concrete over me — not even of wood. Naturally I had known this would be so, but between knowing and experiencing there is a big difference! Shaking all over I waited for the next bomb strike. It didn't come.

"Stay under cover!" Haberzettel ordered — not a moment too soon. There was a roaring sound above like that of a whole convoy of jeeps with hopped-up engines. Two — four — five American long-range fighter planes, which had overtaken the escort convoy of the bombers. At murderous speed they dived down only a few meters above the treetops. Whistling horribly the shells spurted out of their cannon and machine guns. A burst of fire sent great masses of earth spurting up from our trench.

Our 8.8 was silent. The gunners must have had to flatten themselves on the ground. Against low-flying aircraft the 8.8 was useless.

Suddenly I heard a scream and turned, fearfully. I saw the reason; the forest was ablaze. The Americans had thrown down phosphorus. I saw Gerngross pushing himself up out of the trench.

"Stay down, you idiot!" bellowed the corporal, but he was too far from Gerngross to stop him.

Two more pursuit planes flew over. Gerngross must have lost his head because he swung himself over the edge of the trench and ran off. Hardly two paces behind him the bomb struck into the ground.

I was paralyzed with horror and could do nothing but stare after Gerngross. It had happened like lightning!

Suddenly another figure leaped from the trench. It was Point-five! With a speed of which I would never have believed him capable, he threw himself on the little fool and pushed him down to the ground. Gerngross struggled like a maniac until Point-five gave him an uppercut. Then the boy collapsed and lay still. Point-five pulled him up, dragged him back to the trench and rolled into it with the unconscious youngster.

Again I held my breath. The howling of the pursuit planes sounded in the distance, and another bomber squadron flew over us. Again our guns fired. On the very spot where Point-five had stopped Gerngross a bomb fell. Clumps of earth came down on my helmet. The corporal yelled something, but I could not make out what it was. A second bomb struck behind us; a detonation from our gun followed the crash of the bomb — and the fight was over. For a time the crackling of flames was the only sound, then the place came to action.

The firefighters began their work, stretcher bearers hurried to the guns, commands rang out, and where the fire did not light up the place, cones of light from flashlights and torches moved over the ground.

We huddled in the trench, not daring to leave it. Gerngross was still unconscious. Point-five rubbed his head.

"Go to bed, kids," Corporal Haberzettel said, "this is enough for the present. Out here we can manage without you."

My legs felt leaden; it was all I could do to crawl out of the trench. Two stretcher bearers were carrying a wounded man to the shelter where the assistant doctor was stationed. Soon afterward two others brought Private Wittmann. The doctor would not be able to do anything for him — he was dead. A machine gun shell had got him. His dream of going to the Front would never be fulfilled.

We trailed into the barracks and threw ourselves onto the bunks. Point-five came with us and looked after Gerngross.

After a while Bayer asked, "Where did Nero stay?"

Point-five ignored the nickname. "The headmaster was needed in the shelter," he explained without any indication of sarcasm.

I cocked an eye at Schroeder. He lay on his bunk, chewing his fingernails. Apparently he was deep in thought. Walter Müller was on the bunk above me. He bent over and asked hesitatingly, "Do you think that they — came through safely, Gabriel?"

"Who, Walter?"

"Your mother, mine, and — Karin."

"They surely were in the shelter. The ceiling could stand a lot."

"Perhaps our section was spared this time, what do you think?"

What could I answer? I was silent.

"Poor devil," Walter murmured.

"Who?"

"Wittmann." Walter drew back into his bunk with a deep sigh.

Gerngross regained consciousness, and Point-five lifted him up. He waved off the little fellow's thanks. "Behave yourself," he said and left.

Half an hour later the corporal appeared. "I take it that none of you are sleeping," he said in the darkness. "I'll tell you quickly what happened here. Three men were wounded, but the doctor hopes to save them. Wittmann dead. Some damage to two of the guns, which will be repaired by tomorrow. Fire under control. The barracks weren't hit. An enemy bomber was shot down by battery three — with the last shell that was fired. We'll know tomorrow what damage was done in the city. Don't worry about it; the alarm came in time for everyone to get into the shelters."

He walked over to Gerngross. "Lost your nerve, huh?"

The boy didn't answer.

"Be grateful to your teacher," Haberzettel continued, "and next time act more sensibly, please!"

"Yes, Corporal," Gerngross answered in a small voice.

"Good night, all of you."

"Good night, Corporal."

Haberzettel did not go to bed. He hurried out to the emplacement to make himself useful. . . .

Reveille at six o'clock. We jumped out of bed. Only Bayer dawdled; he could have slept much longer. Washing, eating, line-up. Morning exercises were canceled.

The forest fire had been extinguished, but it was

left to us gunners to clear up the last traces of the attack. We filled in the bomb craters, cleared away the broken branches, shoveled dirt and rubble out of the trenches. The corporal and Point-five worked with us.

Suddenly Nero appeared, dressed in civilian clothes. "Always work with a will, men," he encouraged us. "Show yourselves and me and the world that you can hold your ground." Haberzettel muttered something that sounded like "Slacker!"

If Nero heard it, he knew enough not to show it. "I wish I could have been with you gunners last night, but I was needed in the command post."

"In the shelter, sir?" Bayer inquired shamelessly.

Nero's face looked like an overripe tomato. "Continue with your work," he barked and hurried away.

Haberzettel grinned, but Point-five asked, "Do you know what a diplomat is, Bayer?"

"I think so, Doctor."

"Good. A diplomat you are not, my friend. I would advise you to control your tongue better — for your own good."

Bayer stuck his spade into the ground. "Until

yesterday evening I thought that wherever there was danger, a political leader naturally belonged in the middle of it."

"Naturally." The way Point-five said it, he clearly meant the opposite. I looked at Schroeder. He lowered his eyes and began to shovel furiously.

A quarter of an hour later Lieutenant Vogt came. "All listen!" He brought news from the city; the devil knows where he had picked it up. The area around the railroad station had been hard hit as well as some of the older parts of the city. The part we lived in was not damaged. I sighed with relief. Nothing had happened to Mother. Walter Müller looked over at me smiling.

The identity of the bomber which had been shot down by our battery could not be determined. No one had bailed out; the men and the machine were inextricably mixed in one mass of debris.

Toward midday we finished the work and attended the burial of Private Wittmann. First Lieutenant Vollmer gave the eulogy, then the clods of earth fell. Private Heller put a birch cross on the grave with Wittmann's helmet on the top. The grave was close to the gun where Wittmann had fallen.

No Latin or math in the afternoon; other things were now more important. The corporal gave us combat training, and the lieutenant drilled us in gunnery. Special duty came next for individual groups. Gerngross and Hauschild: telephone training. Thumser and Huber: instruction on the range finders. Müller and Schneider: sound locator. Schroeder, Braun, and Schmidt: manipulation of the searchlight. Bayer, Korner, and I: special drill as gun loaders. Point-five was with us. He was being trained as a gun pointer.

"Attention, everyone!" Nero inspected the various groups, praised where according to him the work went well, and reprimanded where it was clumsily done.

Our instructor cast baleful glances after him when he left. "That guy could make himself useful in other ways than by snuffling around in matters about which he doesn't know anything," Private Heller growled near me. I learned something new: a brown uniform doesn't necessarily guarantee that the wearer is a real fighter for folk and fatherland.

In the evening I read the army despatch which hung on the classroom blackboard. It made me certain that the Führer would have to hurry with that secret weapon. The Russians had won territory in the east. One sentence was given to the attack on our city: "Damage was sustained in a residential district." Müller tapped me on the shoulder. "Horrible, Gabriel, isn't it? Residential district! That means women and children and the wounded in the hospitals."

"The Führer will use the secret weapon."

"Soon, I hope," Walter answered. "I prefer to be here upon earth, not like Wittmann, under it."

When we went to dinner, we saw the wounded being taken away to a military hospital. One of them, not too badly hurt, said cheerfully, "Going home to Mother! This filthy war is over for Gunner Jokisch!" He sounded happy.

I was afraid of being wounded, but I would not cringe if hell broke loose again. I wore a blue-gray uniform and felt not only fear but duty. I did not want to be like Nero. Blue-gray was stronger than brown!

The food tasted flat, although Bayer insisted that it was oversalted. . . .

Following the attacks which cost Wittmann his life came several peaceful days and quiet nights.

This did not mean, however, that we could be idle. There was always work to be done in the camp. Instruction about equipment and guns, military training, terrain, school lessons, rifle, pistol, and machine gun shooting — instruction, training, instruction. . . . Now as before we saw very little of First Lieutenant Vollmer, only occasionally at roll call. He received the reports, greeted us, we answered. That was all.

Lieutenant Vogt proved to be a good superior, Haberzettel a rough diamond who was tough but never unfair. When Nero appeared, the corporal screwed up his face; he got along well with Point-five. I saw the two together often.

With Nero it was another story. "I think he came here because he feels safer in the concrete shelter than in the cellar at home," Barbarossa guessed. I didn't contradict him. That may have been the reason. But I had learned from Schroeder of another.

Schroeder was always alone. Since the row the others didn't persecute him, but they avoided him. I exchanged a few words with him now and then, but came no closer. Most of the time I spent with

Müller and Thumser. We didn't settle any world problems, but we got along well together. As to Nero we were of one mind. Since the attack we no longer regarded him as our model even though he had let up on the Latin.

Among the regulars there were those who showed various degrees of enthusiasm, also the dull, the indifferent, the grumblers. They kept to themselves and had nothing to do with us, yet occasionally I caught words that scared me.

I should have reported these men, but I thought of Nero and Schroeder and decided not to. At the time of the attack all of us had stood by one another. We were one big family which consisted of good, bad, and average children. (Haberzettel had said this, and it hit the mark.) And like a family we stuck together when the need came.

"We'll show our teeth to the common enemy even though we want Father to go to the devil," said one sergeant major of the third battery. I knew whom he meant by "Father." Our corps leader, and Nero for sure, would denounce this man as an enemy of the people, a traitor. The sergeant major wore the Iron Cross, First and

Second Class, and the silver wound pin. He had a wife and three children somewhere in the Ruhr district.

Perhaps I was too suspicious. After all, by Father mightn't he have meant the war? Of course! Strange that I hadn't thought of it right away. Here people didn't weigh every word. Soldiers talked a rough language anyway. They used expressions which would have made my mother faint, and some of the experiences they boasted of . . .

A despatch from the High Command admitted that American and British planes were these days bombarding Munich, Münster, Cologne, Dortmund, Coblenz, Wilhelmshaven, Berlin, Hamburg, Stralsund, Stettin, and places in Silesia.

Lieutenant Vogt and Corporal Haberzettel drilled us in practice alarms. They took special care with our machine gun training. "One good shot brings down two out of three low-flying pursuit planes," Vogt declared.

Then came the affair of Gerngross. It was on an evening in the middle of October, shortly before suppertime. Lieutenant Vogt took Gerngross to the officers' barracks. He did not return for supper. We made all sorts of guesses and were agreed on one point only: it must be something bad — the lieutenant looked so serious. Later, when Gerngross returned, Point-five came with him. Haberzettel was in the next barracks playing skat; so we gunners were alone in the room. Gerngross was as pale as death. "Lie down," Point-five said gently to the boy. "Tomorrow morning we'll go together."

Gerngross nodded weakly. "Thank you, Doctor." He threw himself on the bed and buried his face in his hands. Dr. Winkler turned to us. "Leave him in peace. He needs it." He nodded to us and left.

His warning held our questions back. We sat silently and stared at Gerngross. He was a sad sight, with his hands pressed against his eyes, his whole body shaking with soundless sobs. The silence was oppressive. Just to break it, I said the first thing that occurred to me: "What do you think the secret weapon will look like?"

At that Gerngross jumped up so violently that he hit his head on the upper bunk. He didn't seem to feel it. With two strides he came to the table. "Man, Briel," he screamed, "are you really so stupid or do you take us for fools?"

We had never seen him so angry. Even Long Bayer was speechless. What had changed the quiet boy, who usually went out of his way to avoid disputes? He gave the answer without being asked.

"Secret weapon! What a laugh that is! We are the secret weapon, do you hear? We gunners and the girls, the auxiliaries they've had for the last few weeks in the other batteries. Secret weapon! You won't fool anybody with that if he has any brains in his head, Briel. Where could this marvelous thing be built without the English and Americans blasting it with their bombs?"

I was shocked. Gerngross had never seemed gloomy, but now he was talking like the people Nero called alarmists, cowards, and traitors. The little fellow must have lost his mind. Of course he was wrong.

"What's the matter, Gerngross?" Josef Schneider laid his hand on the boy's shoulder. . . . He shook it off, his eyes blazing.

"Don't worry!" he shouted, "I haven't cracked my skull. I won't panic any more when the bombs crash either. But I can't stand the agitators who sound off about heroism, then crawl into hiding-places when the chance to be a hero comes. There are a whole lot of Neros. I wouldn't get my brains knocked out for them, not on your life! Only for the women and children and the old people who huddle in shelters in the city. With every bomber that we shoot down we save some of them, perhaps. The rest can go to the devil!"

We stared at the little fellow as if he were a ghost. Still with tears in his eyes, he laughed grimly. "Even early today I was as keen as you — I really was — until the lieutenant came for me. Listen! Yesterday evening my mother was torn to pieces by a dud bomb that exploded as she was going home from the munitions factory. Nobody knows why the bomb had not been found earlier or why it exploded at just the moment when my mother was going by. The lieutenant learned about it from a sergeant major who had returned from the city; that's why he took me to the officers' barracks. Tomorrow I have leave to go to the city for my mother's funeral. Point-five and Nero were there when Vogt told me about it. Both the lieutenant and Point-five behaved just right. They said very little and pressed my hand. But Nero —"

The little fellow's voice faltered. "Nero made a speech!— all about proud grief, the stiff upper lip, and the honor it is for a German woman to sacrifice her life in the people's battle. He really did, and perhaps you understand me better now. I hate the murderers in the bombers, but I also hate those who have dumped us into the soup!"

Overcome with anger and grief, Gerngross threw himself on the bunk and cried like a child. Otto Thumser went to him and stroked his hair. Gerngross didn't resist.

Schroeder left the room. Then I saw red. I ran after him and grabbed him by the collar, not five steps away from the barracks. "Listen to me, Schroeder," I panted, "when someone loses his mother suddenly, he can be so upset that he doesn't know what he is saying. Of course Gerngross is wrong; it would be terrible if he really meant it. But if you squeal to Nero, I'll break every bone in your body!"

Schroeder shoved me back. His voice trembled. "How could you believe that I'd be such a swine? I don't intend to go to Nero; I came out to be alone. I've got to do some thinking, Briel, in case you know what that is. I'm not going to squeal on Point-five or Vogt either if they make a slip. Now leave me alone!"

"I'm sorry, Schroeder," I muttered, and held out my hand to him. He ignored it, left me standing there, and went slowly toward the woods. But I heard him say to himself, "An honor for a German woman — the devil!"

✠ 6 ✠

The Middle of October, 1944

WEEKEND LEAVE until Sunday afternoon, in uniform. This time Bayer, Bubi, and I were the lucky ones.

It should be a real celebration. I was overjoyed to see Mother again and surprise her. And I didn't go empty-handed. As soldiers, we were not accustomed to luxuries, but we did have enough to eat. We didn't have to use ration stamps. For a feast with Mother I had saved up a whole loaf of bread, a jar half-filled with jam, and — what I was proudest of — two bars of chocolate. Besides, I had scrounged two packages of cigarettes, which Mother could exchange for food.

On Saturday at ten we drove off. Private Hahn from our battery drove the truck with Private Schmoll beside him. Private Heller sat in the rear with Long Bayer, Hauschild and me. Heller was number one gunner of the double-barreled machine gun which was mounted on the movable gun-carriage. Vogt had appointed me number two gunner. I was responsible for the supply of ammunition.

We felt carefree and all went well. No plane appeared in the sky. Bayer, Bubi and I got off near our school. The privates drove on to load up with ammunition. At four o'clock on Sunday afternoon they would pick us up again at the school.

We three separated; my way was the shortest. I was relieved to see that nothing had happened to our district in the last air raid. That here and there paper instead of glass was in the window frames was nothing unusual. The blasts of the explosions affected a wide area, and glass was in short supply.

My mother embraced me as if we had not seen each other for an eternity. She had come back only a few minutes before from the munitions factory where for several months she had been doing her compulsory service. Gunner Briel no longer existed. I was Mother's son and glad to be at home. She was delighted with the gifts, but wondered anxiously whether I had deprived myself too much. She did not mourn the "unnecessary" cabinet which she had chopped to pieces and now used for firewood.

As if we had agreed upon it, we didn't talk about the war. I would not burden her with what gave me a heavy heart. Wittmann, Nero, and Gerngross were far away. They should, for the time being at least, remain so.

Father had not yet written. "A letter can be weeks in coming because of the distance," I tried to console Mother.

"Or lost," she said. "We'll hope for the best." She was pretending. I knew she was very worried, and so was I.

The dinner tasted good, although Mother could prepare only a vegetarian meal of potatoes and carrots since her meat ration stamps were used up. For dessert we had bread and jam. We didn't let it bother us that the jam was made partly of turnips; I ate even the hard, dry bread with a good appetite. Gunner Briel was not ashamed that he felt well and safe with his mother.

In the afternoon I wanted to visit some friends,

with Mother of course. We ought to be together in the little time we had. "Can we drop in on the Beckers?" I asked. I was thinking less of Mr. and Mrs. Becker than of the fox terrier, Fiffi. The Beckers were friends of my parents, had often visited us, and I had taught Fiffi many tricks. They lived scarcely twenty minutes away from us.

Mother shook her head. "They were bombed out and have gone to live with relatives in the country."

"Not — not injured?" I stammered.

"Thank God, no. Their own lives and some important papers in a trunk in the shelter were all that they could save. Fiffi was off somewhere during the attack; he hasn't come back."

"And — the Franks?" They were an old couple to whom I was attached because they used to give me something good to eat after I had been playing handball.

"Dead," said Mummy. "They were with others in an air-raid shelter when a mine crashed through the top. No one came out alive."

I swallowed, "Perhaps we can go to — to the Behrendts?" Adolf Behrendt was two years younger than I and had gone only to elementary school, but I was friendly with him. We had often exchanged stamps.

Again Mother shook her head. "Better not, Gustav. Mrs. Behrendt is not likely to be at home. Adolf is in the hospital. He was badly burned after the air raid when he helped to put out a fire. They had dropped phosphorus bombs. Mrs. Behrendt visits her son as often as she can. Since her husband was killed in action —"

"Killed?"

"Yes, Gustav. Mrs. Behrendt received word a few days ago."

"The Brunner family?"

"Bombed out."

"Krugers?"

"Bombed out."

"Old Mrs. Meyer with whom I sometimes went shopping?"

"She had gotten so she could hear almost nothing, Gustav; so she knew of the alarm too late. Then she couldn't move fast enough."

"Dead?"

Mother nodded.

"Müllers?" I continued hurriedly and sensed

that I was blushing. "I know their house is standing. I came by there. Walter asked me to give them his love."

"On my way home from work I met Walter's mother and sister. Mrs. Müller said she was taking Karin to stay with her grandparents in the country."

I gave up.

Mother put her hand on my arm. "Some things have changed since you went away, Gustav — unfortunately not for the better."

I clenched my hands. "It won't last very much longer, Mother."

"Until everything is destroyed, Gustav?"

I looked at her with dismay and noticed suddenly the wrinkles in her face. Mother had become old! — old and tired before her time. I felt sorry for her and controlled my temper. As calmly as I could, I answered, "Everywhere in the country young people like us are called up for home defense. We make it possible for the trained soldiers to go to the Front. The enemy will find that out. And when the Führer gives the order for the use of the secret weapon —"

Mother interrupted me. "I thought that you had stopped believing in that fairy tale, Gustav."

"Mother!"

"This is the truth. The English and Americans are in control of the air over our country, and there is hardly one of the larger cities that has not been bombed. They are always getting reinforcements from overseas, whereas our reserves are coming to an end."

"Our V-1 and V-2 fly constantly over London!" I said with heat.

"London is not England and certainly not America. Do you hear the army reports?"

"Of course, Mother, there is a radio in our room."

"Then you must have heard that there is a ring around Germany that grows tighter every day. The slight advances that we succeed in making have only prestige value, which does not justify the sacrifices required."

We had not wanted to talk about the war, but now we were doing it. "What do you really want, Mother?"

"That you open your eyes, my dear!"

"I am not blind!"

"You wear blinders, Gustav; that is bad enough."

"You talk like Gerngross!" I protested. "But you are no more right than he."

"What about Gerngross?"

I told her reluctantly. When I finished, Mother looked at me for a long time, then asked, "Why did you not report him?"

"None of us reported him," I answered stiffly. "We certainly would not be guilty of that because if we did, he —" I stopped short.

"He — what, Gustav?"

"He would get into trouble," I answered crossly.

"Trouble!" Mother laughed bitterly. Suddenly she got up, took her coat, and said, "Come!"

"Where, Mother?"

"We are going for a walk through the city, Gustav. There are many new things to see."

I was glad that this talk had stopped. It was getting on my nerves.

"Okay!" I put on my coat and helped Mother. Her coat had become very shabby; cloth had been hard to get for a long time. And winter was coming!

"When I become a big shot, Mother, I'll buy you a fur coat — a Persian lamb or a mink," I said, jokingly.

"Come, we don't want to lose any time, son."

The streetcar stop was only a few meters away from our house. I was glad that the cars still ran; their rattle meant life. There could be no talk of a dead city. The two cars were already filled, but with some pushing and shoving we got two places to stand. An old conductress pushed her way through to us and gave us tickets. She looked grouchy.

In front of me sat a man holding a crutch on his knees. "It's a shame," he growled with an irritated glance at me. "Now they think that green boys have grown up enough to bite the dust for the fatherland. Soon they'll be taking the cripples!"

Suddenly it became very quiet in the car. The rattling of the wheels sounded all the louder.

"And you call yourself a German?" a young woman sneered.

The man with the crutch nodded to her. "My youngest was seventeen and gunner's helper like that one there. He got caught in the last attack. His left leg and right foot amputated, my friends, and my own leg became stiff in Russia. Do you want to see my identity card so that you can inform against me?"

The woman said no more.

In the other corner someone was telling a stale joke, and a few people laughed uproariously. At the next stop the woman got off. Mother said nothing: she left me to my thoughts.

A platoon leader and an ordnance sergeant got on and again it was quiet for a while in the car. Then a few scraps of conversation were resumed.

The ride became slower. Outside, ruins slid by; it was difficult to keep the streetcar line free of debris. Men, women, and children were working in the rubble. A little girl, beaming with delight, tightly clasped a broken doll which she had pulled out of a pile of rubbish.

During the last attack the Party Headquarters had been hit. In one place national guardsmen were cleaning up, in another prisoners of war supervised by soldiers. Now and then trucks and motorcycles rolled by, driven either by uniformed men or party men in brown. And everywhere there were old men, women, and children with little handcarts, dragging what few possessions they had been able to salvage.

I should have liked to slap my own face. Everywhere I was seeing only the seamy side. Had I become a sissy, letting myself be influenced by my mother? Defiantly I told myself: the enemy can not defeat us until they have torn off the last stone!

The streetcar stopped. The terminus was a bomb crater. On the left had stood a factory which had been the special target of the enemy bombs during the last attack. It was demolished. Parachute mines had exploded in the street, which would be impassable for a long time. Auxiliary troops were pushing rubble into the yawning crater.

"We have arrived," Mother said quietly. Now I understood. One of the large cemeteries was here. Mother led me in. Bombs had destroyed some graves, but this was not why she had brought me here. Farther on, I saw bouquets, branches of pine, and a few official wreaths with black, white and red ribbons.

"The dead from the last attack. Read, son."

On some of the new mounds there were names and numbers. I read and shuddered. In one grave lay an entire family, the Niederlechners, killed in a single moment: Anton, 81; Maria, 79; Friedrich Wilhelm, 53; Therese, 48; Brigitte, 22; Hans, 13; Helmut, 11; Liselotte, 7; Gabriella and Gisela, 4.

Death from the air had become stronger than the roofs of the shelters. . . . I sighed with relief when we left the cemetery. My glance fell on the wall of a ruin on which white letters stood out vividly: "Our walls you can break, our hearts never!" Mother saw me lingering but hurried me on.

We had only a short distance to go. The ruins of bombed houses had been cleared away enough to provide a narrow footpath. People coming toward us were in a hurry, scarcely any of them greeted us.

Mother was taking me to the neighborhood of the munitions factory where she worked. The building had been only slightly damaged; production still went on. About three hundred meters behind the factory there was a wooden hut, enclosed by barbed wire. It was a prison for the Serbians who had been captured in the war and who worked in the factory. Behind the barbed wire a chestnut tree lifted leafless branches to the sky. On one of the lowest a man hung. His hands were tied behind his back and a placard was fastened on his chest. I clenched my teeth.

"A Serbian prisoner of war," Mother said. "They hanged him last evening. The placard reads, 'I have made use of the blackout to steal the property of the German people.' In German and Serbian, Gustav. The poor devil was hungry, and a patrol caught him when he was burrowing in the rubble of a bombed house. Unluckily for him he had found a coat. For this theft and his absence without permission from the prison he was condemned to death. As a warning they have placed him on exhibition."

I turned my eyes away. "Who sentenced him?"

"Some court or other. They sentenced him in the name of the German people."

"Let's go home," I begged.

"The sentence was given on order of the Führer," Mother continued. "That man is not the first, nor will he be the last."

I ran. Mother followed me slowly. I stopped only when a heap of rubble shut off the terrible sight. "Why did you show me that?" I asked when she caught up with me.

"So that you would finally open your eyes!"

Then her voice sounded warm and motherly again. "I don't want to lose you, my son! You should get over this nonsense. Look, one of these days, instead of English and American bombers, enemy tanks will attack our city. Make for safety then as fast as you can. For Heaven's sake, don't be one of those who want to fight to the last breath. Their sacrifice is senseless. You must live, Gustav, do you hear? For your own sake — and mine!"

I could not answer. The idea that enemy tanks would attack us was too horrible. On the way back Mother and I did not speak again. At home I threw myself on the sofa, shut my eyes — then opened them at once. I dared not keep them closed because then I saw the chestnut tree behind the barbed wire and heard a rasping voice roar out of the dark: "In the name of the people!"

Mother turned on the radio. March music! I jumped up and turned it off. "What about a game of chess?" She was willing. Although she didn't play well, I was even worse today than she was. I barely managed to hold the game to a draw; otherwise Mother would have checkmated me.

That night there was no air-raid alarm so we didn't go into the shelter. Sunday morning a loud

singing woke me. Eight o'clock already! I jumped
out of bed, opened the window and looked down.
A troop in field gray was marching by, young men
with officers' stripes on their sleeves and a skull on
their caps. They sang:

> *When everything is smashed,*
> *We will still be marching.*
> *Today our country hears us —*
> *Tomorrow all the world!*

Behind them a paratrooper with a gold wound
stripe crossed the street, led by a Red Cross nurse.
His eye sockets were empty . . .

Mother and I talked no more about the war. We
spoke of the past and built castles in the air for the
future. The hours flew. When I left, Mother said,
"Good luck, my son." I noticed that she was holding back tears, and went quickly.

Bayer and Bubi were already at the school when
I got there. The truck came a few minutes later,
and we were off. Private Hahn drove with Private
Schmoll dozing beside him. He had somehow
found a bottle of schnapps and had wiped out his
problems with alcohol. Heller sat with us in the

back, whistling and drumming the rhythm on his gunstock. We three were silent; Bayer and Hauschild were probably thinking of home, as I was.

The city was behind us, and then it happened. Sirens howled!

"Damned swine!" growled Heller, and raised the binoculars to his eyes. Hahn stepped on the gas in an effort to reach the woods before the bombs fell.

"Now they're coming by daylight!" Long Bayer shouted.

"Stop your noise!" ordered Heller.

The railroad line was near the street on which we were tearing along. On it ran a train which had just left the station to escape the bombardment of the city, according to instructions. We were going full speed ahead when, scarcely fifty meters from the woods, the truck's motor stopped. Panic! The privates swore, and we did, too. Hahn and the now-sobered Schmoll tore the hood up and looked feverishly for the trouble. Heller stood behind the machine gun, like a beast of prey ready to spring.

"Scram!" he yelled at us three. "I'll handle this alone. Get under cover in the woods." We jumped off. Pressed against the ground, I looked first at the sky, then at the truck on which Hahn and Schmoll worked desperately.

Then came blow after blow. From the northwest they were whistling in on us, and already waves of fire were crackling.

Bombers!

American fighter bombers! Two — three — five! A short distance from us they plummeted down. Bursts of fire from their cannon poured onto the railroad train. Then I gasped with relief as the whistling died out in the distance.

Hahn and Schmoll had kept on working, hardly stopping to look up when they realized that the attack hadn't got us. Heller hadn't fired, probably because he didn't want to call the bombers' attention to the truck.

Hope fled again. Two more planes roared overhead, and this time it was in earnest. Somewhere antiaircraft guns were firing, but I couldn't see where because of the clouds of smoke. Near us clumps of earth shot up and a shell shattered the left side of the truck. Schmoll and Hahn lay flat on the ground. Heller shot back. The track of the tracer bullets hissing from the barrels could be clearly followed. The planes swung off and made a loop. Schmoll jumped onto the truck beside Heller. Hahn stayed under cover.

Second attack! Schmoll ripped shells out of the case and Heller . . . I pressed my hand against my mouth in horror. Heller flew out of the truck as if a giant fist had knocked him to the ground. Schmoll fell to the floor of the truck and pressed his hand against his left shoulder.

The bombers circled off. Hahn jumped up. "Take Schmoll to the camp!" he yelled and got busy again on the engine. Long Bayer was already on the way, and I followed him without thinking, acting instinctively. Hauschild ran behind me. One look was enough: Heller was dead, Schmoll wounded.

"Come, Gabriel," Bayer gasped. We lifted Schmoll by his hands and feet without stopping to bandage him. There was no time, for the roars were returning above. The bombers were starting their third attack. Hardly knowing what I was doing I let go of Schmoll, who was groaning with pain, jumped onto the truck, and shouted to Bayer, "Ammunition!" Hauschild threw himself under cover.

I pulled back the trigger and fired at random against the planes, which were zooming down fast. Only when Bayer pushed another shell toward me did I realize that the planes had us under fire. Then I pulled the trigger again. Fragments flew from the left wing of the second plane.

The fight was over. Reaction followed, and I passed out. When I came to, the truck was already bumping its way through the forest. Bayer and Hauschild crouched near me; Heller and Schmoll were lying on the floor. Schmoll had been bandaged in a makeshift fashion.

"Well!" Bayer grinned. "Gabriel is with us again!" I noticed that he had been hurt too, for his left hand was bandaged. He made little of it. "A clean shot," he said casually, trying to conceal the pain.

"And — the bomber — with the smashed wing?" I asked hoarsely.

Bayer made a wry face. "I'm not sure that you brought it down, little Briel, but it could be." Then he groaned, and fell backwards.

In the camp we attracted little attention. The assistant doctor took care of Schmoll and Bayer, dressed their wounds, and had them sent to the military hospital. He could do nothing for Heller, who was buried beside Wittmann.

Hahn gave our news to the regulars. He must have told an absurd tale, for on Monday early the commanding officer of the Second Division appeared, made a speech, and decorated me with the Iron Cross, Second Class. Bayer also received it; Lieutenant Vogt was to give it to him in the hospital.

My comrades said, "Hearty good wishes!" or "You're a crazy kid!" or "You earned it!"

Lieutenant Vogt's only comment was, "If you had aimed a little better you would have got the Iron Cross, First Class."

Corporal Haberzettel, "Now that's not bad for a start." Nero slapped my shoulder. "I am proud of you, Assistant Gunner Briel. You have performed an act worthy of a German! Strong in loyalty!"

"Higher mathematics," is the way Point-five put it, and when I looked at him puzzled:

"Two fighter bombers, two assistant gunners, one machine gun, two Iron Crosses, Second Class.

"Remainder: one dead, two wounded, one damaged truck."

Even when I was not yet wearing the blue-gray

uniform, I had wanted nothing more than to get a medal. Now I could not be really happy about it. The "remainder" weighed too heavily.

The armed forces report announced briefly: "Low-flying planes launched an attack against the civilian population in west and southwest Germany." Our city was in the south.

On the following night I could not get to sleep for a long time; so I heard the drone in the distance.

Bombers!

Yet no alarm was given. The noise droned off southwards, toward Salzburg, the city of Mozart. In our opera house, which now lay in ruins, I had once seen *The Magic Flute*. I shuddered now, hearing the beat of kettle drums which had nothing to do with Mozart.

✠ 7 ✠

The Second Half of October, 1944

A WEAKER ENEMY combat squadron had attacked our city. The defense was hampered since the enemy prevented us from discovering his position by dropping strips of tinfoil. Our range finder picked up the strips as flying objects just as it did the bombers.

On the return flight the planes came over our position without dropping bombs. We fired from all the batteries. I stood as gun loader at the 8.8 and shivered like a hunting dog when the searchlight picked out a bomber. We shot down a four-engined plane, the shells tore it to pieces in the air. None of the crew bailed out. Next morning Corporal Haberzettel painted a new ring around the gun barrel.

In the forenoon we had stiff training at the battery and in the afternoon a Latin class that was as different from Ovid as decency is from vulgarity. Nero had gone to the city and returned about half an hour before the lesson. When he came into the classroom in his party uniform, his manner boded ill. "Thumser!"

Otto sprang up and stood at attention. "Here, sir!"

"I have sad news for you, Thumser," said Nero indifferently.

The boy trembled and lost his self-control. He spoke without permission. "Is it something about my mother, sir? Was she — during the attack — I mean —"

"Silence!" Nero's voice rang sharply.

"Yes, sir." I felt sorry for Otto when I looked at Nero's mean face. I hated him. The others were staring at him too. Nero seemed to enjoy each word. "At our conference today the district leader informed me that a certain Anna Thumser of 11 Hermann Goering Street — that is your mother?"

"Yes, sir."

". . . That this Anna Thumser was accused by the air-raid warden of her house of listening to an enemy broadcasting station. At the trial the accused made a full confession. She has been imprisoned."

I could see Thumser trembling and trying to control the quivering of his lips. His face was gray.

"I know that you are an honorable person, Thumser," Nero continued, "and I hope that you will have nothing to do with one who has behaved so traitorously. Answer!"

"What will happen to my mother?" Otto stammered.

"Undermining the fighting spirit is a crime deserving the severest punishment," said Nero coldly. "And now your answer! This is a command!"

Thumser collapsed. He sank on the bench, put his face in his hands, and didn't move.

Who first began to stamp his feet could not be discovered, but we all stamped together.

Nero grew red. "Quiet!" he roared. We continued to stamp until Thumser cried, "No!" Then it was deathly still.

"Take him out, Briel," Nero commanded, and to Schroeder, "You come with me."

"I don't want to, sir," Schroeder answered, to my surprise. He put his hand over his mouth, but I was quite close to him and saw that he did not look at all as if he would break down.

"Good for you, Schroeder!" I whispered.

"Get out of here!" Nero shouted angrily. Schroeder left the classroom quickly.

"Briel, take Thumser away!"

Otto still cowered on the bench. I took his arm. "Come, I'll stay with you." He let himself be led away. As I pushed the door shut with my foot I heard Nero saying, "All right! Now let's see whether you are as good at Latin as you are at stamping your feet. Ovid, page nine, second sentence. Begin, Braun."

"The swine!" Thumser groaned, "the damned swine!"

"I'll talk with Point-five and Lieutenant Vogt," I promised. "They'll help you."

Thumser shook his head, threw himself on the bunk, and sobbed. "I don't believe it, Gabriel! My mother has never been interested in politics."

"I'll talk first with Point-five, Otto."

He seized my hand and held it fast. "Stay with me, Gabriel, only a few more minutes. And if you believe my mother is bad, don't say so. I'm afraid of what I might do if I were alone."

"All right, Otto, I'll stay."

He lay back and closed his eyes. He didn't say any more, but I could tell by the twitching of his hand how he was suffering. From the classroom next door I heard the voices of the others, but I paid no attention to what they were saying. My thoughts whirled about like pictures in a kaleidoscope. Out of the murmur to which the voices sank, I could hear my father: "Many a one who does not think as we do can be an upright man."

The corps leader: "A German knows no fear."

Father: "Fear is not cowardice. I myself was terrified before the battle in which I won the first Iron Cross."

Lieutenant Vogt: "For a soldier, his honor is to be valued above all else."

Corporal Maier number two: "After years in the service we have had a snootful. It makes me sick!"

Private Wittmann: "If I should be kept from going to the Front on account of you, you won't live to see it!"

Gunner Jokisch after he had been wounded: "For me this filthy war is over!"

First Lieutenant Vollmer: "See to it that you don't behave like babies."

Barbarossa: "I think he came here because he feels safer in the concrete shelter than in the cellar at home."

Mother: "You should get over this nonsense, Gustav! Don't be one of those who want to fight to the last breath!"

Gerngross: "I can't bear the agitators who sound off about heroism, then crawl into a hiding place when the chance to play the hero comes. There are a whole lot of Neros. I wouldn't get my brains knocked out for them, you can bet your life! Only for the women and children and the old people in the city who huddle in shelters in fear of their lives. With every bomber that we shoot down we save some of them, perhaps."

Nero: "For the German woman it is an honor to sacrifice her life in the people's battle."

Gerngross: "I hate the murderers in the bombers, but I also hate those who have dumped us in the soup!"

116

I: "The Führer is always right!"

Mother: "You wear blinders, Gustav! They hanged him yesterday evening . . . in the name of the German people."

Schroeder: "I am supposed to listen and notice who tells jokes about the Führer and the other officials, who spreads enemy propaganda or otherwise undermines the fighting spirit. Then I am to report to him. And — I am to observe closely whether Lieutenant Vogt and Point-five make any remarks which could be considered subversive."

Mother: "Bombed out — dead — badly burned — bombed out — killed in action —"

The men with the skull on their caps: "When everything is smashed, we will still be marching!"

Nero: "That is your mother, isn't it, Thumser? I hope that you will have nothing to do with one who has behaved so traitorously!"

Point-five: "Lie down, Gerngross. Tomorrow we'll go together, won't we?"

The housemaster of our school: "A traitor, this Dr. Winkler!"

Haberzettel to Gerngross: "Be grateful to your teacher."

Zeus: "I have an account to settle."

Point-five: "Higher mathematics."

I gritted my teeth and tried to drown out the voices, then I saw the pictures. Blankly I stared at the barracks window. My father saying good-bye. Only now I realized that he showed no enthusiasm. Knowing the horror of war, he went only because he had to.

Nero: a big shot when he was talking, very small when the bombs were falling, contemptible as a man.

Lieutenant Vogt: career man, a soldier; I had never heard him speak of politics.

Point-five: How I had misjudged him! Not a man of words, but he was there where words do not reach: in the trenches, at the guns, at the salvage work, and wherever anyone needed the consolation that can't be found in empty phrases.

Mother: old before her time, tired and bitter.

I: Yes, where did I really stand?

If I were just the same as I had been three weeks ago, I would have despised Maier number two and Jokisch because they had had a "snootful." For "Our walls you can break, our hearts never!" I would believe that I must agree with every decree made in the name of the people because "The people and the Führer are one!" and "The Führer is always right!"

I would believe that I must inform against alarmists, grumblers, "propagandists destroying the war spirit." For "Whoever by his speech shows that he is not unconditionally behind the Führer and the party stabs our fighting men in the back, fouls the memory of the fallen, and forfeits the right to live in the fellowship of the German people."

How often had I heard these statements proclaimed in the Hitler Youth evening school and how acceptable they seemed to me! But now? Now it was no longer a case of anonymous persons, apathetic, criminal, traitorous. To condemn them then had been easy because I sat in judgment on unknown persons who had already been marked out by their arrest. Now the anonymity no longer existed.

"The Grumbler" — Maier two. "The Criminal" on the chestnut tree behind the barbed wire. "The Destroyers of the war spirit"— Anna

Thumser and Gerngross — even my mother. Yes, she, too. Because of the words she spoke to open my eyes Nero could twist the halter around her neck. Nero! He would not hesitate for a moment to condemn my mother as he had Thumser's, with contemptuous words spoken before all the others.

He is only one, I tried to tell myself. Nero is not the party. But I saw again the man hanging on the chestnut tree; I saw the men who arrested Anna Thumser, I heard the voice of the corps leader: "Whoever shows in his speech . . ." and there droned in my ears: "Command of the Führer!"

I saw the people in the streetcar, saw them become silent when the Home Defense officers got on, and I was aware of their fear. They feared the very ones whom they should trust. "You wear blinders, Gustav," Mother had said.

No more of this! Nero had thrown me off balance. It was a bitter realization. There must be someone to whom I could unburden myself. Not Thumser; he was in too terrible a state himself. Gerngross would understand, Walter Müller also, perhaps, or "the brave little Schneider."

Helmut Schroeder returned. I started as the door shut behind him. Leaning against the wall he said, "You are to go to Point-five, Briel. He is in his room at the officers' barracks."

I stared at him in amazement. "Does that mean that you —?"

Schroeder put his finger on his lips, pointed to Thumser, then at the door to the classroom. "Not so loud, Briel. Go ahead! I have to ask Ammon to take over the next class since Dr. Winkler is having an important conference with Lieutenant Vogt. I met him outside by chance when I — was not feeling well. Hurry up, get going!"

I hesitated. "What shall I say if Nero asks me later where I have been?"

"These swine!" Thumser moaned. "These damned swine! I will —"

"You'll do nothing!" Schroeder broke in. "Leave thinking to those who think sensibly."

"Nero? Perhaps you mean him?" Thumser answered.

"Idiot! Why don't you realize that we want to help you?" That was the right tone to use.

Thumser gritted his teeth. "I'm sorry, Schroeder, I just don't know any more whom I can trust and who is a squealer. Should I go with Gabriel?"

121

Schroeder shook his head. "No, Point-five wants to speak to Briel alone. If you went Nero would smell a rat. On your way, Briel!"

"And what shall I say to Nero?"

"Something will occur to you."

I left, and avoided meeting anyone by slipping behind the barracks. This was the first time I had been in Point-five's room. It was simply furnished with a camp bed, a table, two chairs, locker, wash stand, mirror, a round iron stove, a little bookcase with a few books. On the table was a vase filled with pine branches. There was one picture on the wall: "Coming into Power"— Field Marshal Hindenburg, hand outstretched to Hitler in dark civilian clothes, who was bowing low before the old general and state president.

Point-five sat at a table reading. "There you are now, Briel. Take a seat!" He pointed to the empty chair.

I sat down.

"What's on your mind, Briel?"

"You sent for me, Doctor."

"Bravo, Briel! You're a diplomat. Then it's up to me?" He looked at me searchingly. I held his eye steadily.

"Schroeder was with me."

"I know, Doctor."

"He told me that Thumser's mother had been arrested for listening to an enemy broadcast."

"Dr. Ammon informed us of it a little while ago."

"Schroeder was able to give me very little information," Point-five continued. "He could not stay away from the class too long. But he did tell me that Thumser had gone to pieces. I assumed that you would be with him and not in class; so I sent for you. Will you give me a more complete account?"

"Certainly, Doctor." While I talked Point-five did not take his eyes from me. I felt that he was watching my expression and listening to the tone of my voice. "I have met Thumser's mother a few times," I concluded. "She is a simple woman; it is unthinkable that she would be a traitor. Please help her!"

"Actually you must go to Mr. Ammon, Briel."

"To Nero? He'd like to see her hanged."

"You judge harshly, Briel," Point-five said, calmly.

"You should have seen what he did to Thumser,

and —" I stopped short and turned pale. I must not betray that!

"And?" Point-five did not force an answer from me; he requested it. I hesitated only briefly. If I expected his help, I had to trust him.

"He wanted one of us to spy on you! You and Lieutenant Vogt." I dropped my eyes, not wanting to look in his face.

Point-five was not disturbed. "Yes, I know. Schroeder told me."

I couldn't believe I had heard correctly. "Schroeder?"

"A little while ago when he was with me. I am afraid we have all misjudged him."

"You, too, Doctor?"

"Yes, I, too, but now let us talk about Thumser's mother."

"What do you think could happen to her?"

Point-five shrugged. "That's a matter for the judge to decide. Perhaps she'll be put in a concentration camp."

I knew the word, but I could not imagine what such a place was like. "Is it a sort of penitentiary, Doctor?"

Point-five evaded the question. "Perhaps we can

talk about that later. Just remember: to know too much nowadays is dangerous. As to Thumser's mother, I am not in a position to help her since I am not especially esteemed by the authorities. You would know that from the fact that Mr. Ammon authorized Schroeder to — let us say — watch me. I will speak to Lieutenant Vogt and perhaps also to First Lieutenant Vollmer."

"Thank you, Doctor, but please do it very soon!"

He smiled. "In point-five, you mean? I'll try, Briel."

"Thank you. When may I come again?"

"This evening after supper. And bring Thumser with you."

"Yes, thank you, Doctor." I began to say *"Heil Hitler"* but quickly changed it to good-bye.

When I got back to the barracks, Thumser was still lying on his bunk. He jerked upright when he saw me. "What did he say?"

"He is going to help you, Otto. This evening after supper we are both to go to him."

"I'll never forget what you've done, Gabriel."

"It's okay. We all have to stick together against that one in there."

"He's switched the lessons around for the present. I caught a few words. He's talking about Russian atrocities in the east." He jumped up. "Let's go, Gabriel! I'm not going to let him think he can get me down."

As we entered the classroom, Nero was holding forth about "unimaginable crimes committed by the Red rabble on the Baltic Germans" but broke off on seeing us. "I thought you wanted a chance to cut the class, Briel."

"No, sir, I just didn't want to leave Thumser alone; he was so distressed."

Nero waved that off. "Thumser is a soldier, not a crybaby. As I expected, he has got hold of himself. Sit down."

Schroeder winked at me. I nodded and smiled, but when I realized that Nero was watching us, I pretended to be following his lecture.

"The Baltic Germans, whose love for their native soil kept them from fleeing for safety before the advance of the Red army, endured horrors!" Nero declaimed. "Reliable sources report mass murders of the old, of women and children, rape and torture. Most of the soldiers are drunk and

Germans are free game for them. But we strike back! No pardon for the Reds, even if they surrender! That is the Führer's command. These subhuman creatures must be exterminated just like the traitorous element among us . . ."

He interrupted his discourse, fixed his eyes on Otto and asked sharply, "Are you feeling ill again, Thumser?"

I marveled at Otto. I don't believe I could have controlled myself in the same circumstances. He stood at attention. "I'm all right, sir."

"Excellent. Take your seat."

I heard Thumser grinding his teeth. Schroeder raised his hand. "Something has occurred to me, sir, although it is not really apropos. I read some time ago in a book on Frederick II of Prussia that the court intended to have him marry Maria Theresa of Austria. How would the history of Germany have developed if this union had taken place?"

Wonderful, this Schroeder! His trick worked. Nero was fascinated by historical ifs and buts. He didn't get back to the "traitorous element" but instead reveled in the Prussian and Austrian past.

Thumser threw Schroeder a grateful look. He understood. Nero talked in the "if" vein for the rest of the period.

Haberzettel came in. "Out for shooting practice!"

Lieutenant Vogt was at the 8.8. He hardly looked at Thumser, but he was not so stiff with him as with the rest of us. I assumed that Point-five had already spoken to him.

A half hour later I saw an entirely new side of Nero. He must have taken a walk in the forest. In his hands he held — a crow! The bird struggled feebly. We stared amazed, and Corporal Haberzettel shook his head. "The poor bird has broken a wing," Nero said, his voice full of pity. Carefully he stroked the bird. "Perhaps the doctor can do something for it." He went to the barracks where the assistant doctor lived. Nero as a friend to animals! What kind of soul could this man have?

Shortly after supper Thumser and I reported to Point-five. Otto was sure that his teacher would find a way to spare his mother the worst. That was my doing; I had given him encouragement.

Point-five offered us his two chairs and sat on

128

the bed. "I spoke to Lieutenant Vogt," he began without other introduction. "As an officer he disapproves of the law-breaking that listening to an enemy broadcast represents, but he promised me that he would speak to First Lieutenant Vollmer. He thinks perhaps extenuating circumstances could be pleaded since she is a woman whose husband and oldest son are on active duty, and she has a little daughter to care for."

Thumser drew a deep breath. "Thank you, Doctor!"

Point-five waved away the thanks. "Vogt took me aside right after dinner. He had applied to the chief, who promised to inquire about your mother since you belong to his unit. Actually, as an officer he really should not get mixed up in a nonmilitary matter. Before supper Vogt told me the result. First Lieutenant Vollmer had called up the District Court and learned that your mother's trial had already been held at noon today. The extenuating circumstances were taken into consideration, especially the fact that your mother had not repeated the broadcast information. Therefore she was sentenced to protective custody only, and your sister was taken to relatives in the country."

"Protective custody," Thumser muttered. "Is that — imprisonment, Doctor?"

"Something like that."

"For how long, and where?"

"For two years, Thumser. She was taken away this afternoon. Where, Vollmer could not discover."

"Those swine!" Thumser groaned.

Point-five laid his hand on the boy's shoulder. "Pull yourself together. It's not the worst that could happen; the court could have imposed a far harsher sentence."

"Perhaps death by hanging?"

Point-five nodded. "Just that."

"Doctor, you don't really mean that!" I protested, horrified.

"Life doesn't mean much in our time," he replied. "In a way we are all condemned to death. Whether we shall be reprieved depends upon how long the war lasts."

Thumser gritted his teeth. "I'll ask for leave to go to the city."

"And then?"

"Then I'll grab the air-raid warden, that pig of

a denouncer, by the throat! Then they can do whatever they want to me."

"Hanging or shooting, Thumser?" The calm with which Point-five spoke was frightening.

Thumser bent over the table, his hands covering his face.

"Cry yourself out," Point-five said gently, "but pull yourself together in front of the others."

"Especially in front of Nero," I added. "He has a heart only for crows."

Thumser did not answer. For a while there was silence. "Well, we'd better be going," I suggested finally, only for something to say.

Point-five agreed. "I'm sorry I could do nothing for you, Thumser, but you can still hope. Your mother is alive — that is a great deal."

Thumser wiped his eyes on the sleeve of his jacket. "Thank you, Doctor. And — if I lose my nerve again, may I —?"

Point-five interrupted him. "Yes, Thumser, you must come to me. You know where to find me." He shook hands. "Good night, my boy."

Otto did not say "*Heil* Hitler" nor did I. We said good night and left the barracks.

Outside it was quite dark, but we recognized

the man who came out of the officers' shelter and walked toward the barracks. "Nero!" exclaimed Thumser and spat.

"Let's get away from here," I said softly. "He's the last one I want to meet."

We began to run, then stopped short. The sirens were howling. Air raid! Involuntarily I looked back at Nero. While the barracks were coming alive, he turned and ran as fast as he could back to the shelter.

"All out!" It was the voice of Haberzettel. I pushed Otto ahead. "Come on!" We hurried to our barracks, collided with our comrades coming out, fought our way through, snatched our helmets from the lockers, fastened our belts, and just made it. We lined up with the others as the corporal took the roll.

The wind carried the screams of the sirens from the city.

"Regroup!" Haberzettel ordered, as though this were merely a drill. "Dr. Ammon says that he is ready to take over the telephone service, in case of attack."

"In the shelter!" Barbarossa sneered.

The corporal heard him. "Where else, you jerk? Your job is to keep your mouth shut!"

"Yes, sir."

The regulars had already run to the guns, and Haberzettel was delivering a lecture!

"Gerngross, Hauschild, and Korner to gun one of the second battery. Briel, Thumser, and Schroeder to gun two. Braun and Schmidt, the searchlight. Müller and Schneider, the sound locator. Huber, the range finder. To your places, march!"

We were in the command of Lieutenant Vogt. It did not surprise me at all to see Point-five as gunpointer at my gun.

The searchlight sent its beam into the northwest, and the guns of the batteries spewed out shells. A little later the deep roaring of the planes began. Everything happened at the speed of lightning. We gunners had no time to look around. As fast as we could, we tore the shells out of the cases, placed them upright. Lieutenant Vogt gave the orders for fuse setting and aim.

From the city came the crash of the first bombs, and their fires would soon reveal our position. Our searchlight began to probe the sky. The roar of the planes increased as the head of the bomb squadron circled over us.

"Open fire!"

I worked feverishly. Shell after shell flew through my hands. I felt no fear; it was as though I had become a machine.

The bombers opened their shafts directly over us. Seconds later the place was an inferno. Bombs screamed down, struck the guns, burst with an ear-splitting detonation. Now I was afraid, but I held on. The screech and crash of the bombs was every-where now — before me, behind me to left and right. The earth shook. Explosions in the sky, debris flying about, screams, officers barking commands. I wanted to scream, too, but the scream stuck in my throat. A giant bomb hissed down from the sky.

"Take full cover!" Lieutenant Vogt yelled. I pressed the shell I was holding to my chest and flung myself on the ground. As if struck by light-ning and with thunder in my ears I was hurled up, fell down, lay half-stunned. I heard no more; I had become deafened. Suddenly I felt the heat, but I could not move. I knew only that I was holding something tight and must not let go. I saw fire all around.

Two hands lifted me up, and I let myself be pulled away. It was Point-five. He yelled something that I couldn't understand, and then my eyes told me what he said. He took away the shell I had been clutching. He let me fall, ran off with the shell, and came back with empty hands. He didn't bother with me any more but hurried in the direction of our guns.

I came to gradually and saw that I lay in a trench in front of our barracks. Quiet followed the uproar. The attack on our emplacement had lasted only a few minutes. Gradually the buzzing in my ears stopped and at first faintly, then more clearly, I was able to distinguish noises. Wearily I crawled out of hiding. Hardly thirty meters from our gun the woods were blazing where a giant torch had fallen. An enemy plane shot down! I staggered over to where Lieutenant Vogt was giving commands. He assembled his group not far from the scene of the fire. Still half dazed, I obeyed orders mechanically. Someone pushed a spade into my hands, and I worked madly, cutting and throwing turf onto the fire. After a while I noticed that Gerngross was working beside me. "Where is Thumser?" I yelled.

He shrugged. I didn't ask again. The heat bathed me in sweat and dried my tongue. I shoveled, threw, shoveled, threw, until I keeled over. Someone took me to the barracks. Point-five? Haberzettel? One of the regulars? I didn't know.

The alarm-whistle woke me. It was morning. I had gone to bed fully dressed, and so had the others.

Thumser and Schroeder were missing! The corporal looked bleary-eyed but spoke briskly. "All listen!" At once my heart grew heavy. Haberzettel's face reflected nothing good. "The attack last night hit the center of the city where the railroad station is. Seven enemy planes attacked our batteries. A bomber was shot down by gun two of the second battery, another by gun one of the third battery. Our losses: one truck and a jeep which were in the parking lot and — a sergeant major and a private of the third battery, both killed. Several more in the first and third batteries were wounded."

Haberzettel paused, then with obvious emotion

he continued, "Our second battery mourns the death of Assistant Gunner Schroeder. Assistant Gunner Thumser was among the wounded. A fragment of the enemy plane which was shot down took off his right foot. The wounded were cared for by our doctor and then were driven in the night to the military hospital."

We looked at the floor and Hauschild muttered, "Schroeder would have been at the range finder and Thumser at the searchlight —"

"If Nero hadn't taken over the telephone service," Gerngross completed the indictment.

"Each one fights in his own way," Haberzettel declared, "and there had to be someone for telephone duty. Not everyone is qualified for it. Dr. Winkler had his upper arm torn by a bomb splinter."

"Did he go to the hospital?" I asked, alarmed.

Haberzettel grinned. "No, Briel, he had the arm bandaged and got a tetanus shot. But first he took the shell away from you, kid! That's a dangerous thing where there's a fire."

"Will he be all right?" I demanded.

"Who? Dr. Winkler? There's nothing else wrong with him."

"No, Thumser."

"Oh, yes, there are very good artificial limbs. Stop talking! Get ready! Outside in ten minutes!"

It seemed as though everything happened on that day.

About ten o'clock twelve girls of the auxiliary force arrived. They were to be trained for telephone service and the sound locators. Then shortly after noon seven young soldiers of the regular troops packed their gear. Corporal Maier number two was glad not to be one of them. "They're going to the east front," he informed us. "Most of the antiaircraft gunners who have recently left from around here will be sent against the Russians."

He didn't say where he got this information. I heard it again when I went to the washroom, after dinner. Maier two was there with one of the regular soldiers. They didn't stop talking when I appeared. "Going to the eastern front is about the last thing I want. The Russians have a terrific number of tanks. For every one that gets destroyed, two more roll up. I heard this from a fellow on leave."

Maier two nodded. "I'm with you. I don't like tanks, and I haven't the slightest ambition to get a birch cross put on my grave. It's all right now around here, but in the east they lie all day and night in mud, with the bombs dropping down on them."

"So that they won't order us to the east, how about getting drunk this evening, okay?"

"Okay!" Maier two agreed.

For the first time I was afraid for my father, because of what they said about the east. . . .

Haberzettel's whistle broke into my thoughts. I dried my hands quickly and ran, in order not to be late for roll call.

At eight that evening I took over sentry duty. It was bitingly cold, and I pulled up my coat collar as I went the rounds. About nine o'clock there was a racket in front of the barracks next to ours. Someone was singing off key; someone else was trying to keep him quiet.

> *Rosemarie, haho! Rosemarie, haho*
> *I'm thinking of you only!*

"Man, shut up! Do you want to be put in the clink?" The singer continued:

> *But when the Führer calls,*
> *Then goodbye, Rosemarie!*

"Stop it, you idiot!"

The singer was drunk. With the obstinacy of a drunkard, he bawled, "If the Führer calls, Herbert — hic — for me — hic — he can call until he's black in the face! My Führer — I say — my Führer, Corporal — hic — Maier two has a snootful — hic — get stuck in the mud alone!" The rest was smothered in an angry gurgling. His companion must have put his hand over Maier two's mouth. But the corporal evidently tore it away. He kept on scolding, "The Führer can —!"

There was no more. He gurgled again, then I heard other voices. Several soldiers must have rushed out of the barracks. I was standing near our guns and saw only dim figures in the darkness. On no account would I have left my post. I was anxious not to have seen or heard clearly when the affair was investigated. What Maier two had babbled could cost him his head. I thought of the chestnut tree behind the barbed wire. No, I couldn't bear to have Maier two come to such an end. Damned alcohol!

Now there was silence, but the silence disturbed me more than it relieved me. I had an eerie feeling. However, since nothing else happened I resumed my round. . . . More than half an hour went by. Then I saw a form approaching the guns of the second battery. I tore the gun from my shoulder and released the safety catch.

"Halt — Prince!"

"Eugene!" came the prompt answer. It was Lieutenant Vogt. I clicked my heels and reported: "Gunner Briel on duty. Nothing unusual has happened."

"You slept well, did you, Briel?"

"No, Lieutenant."

"Is your hearing defective?"

"No, Lieutenant."

"You are willing to state that you did not hear Maier two roaring?"

"I did hear him, Lieutenant."

"Well, what nonsense was he yelling?"

"Corporal Maier two was singing, Lieutenant. I think the song about Rosemarie."

"And what else?"

"I couldn't understand the rest; Corporal Maier two didn't speak distinctly, and I was standing some distance away."

"All right, continue your rounds." He went back to the barracks, and a regular relieved me.

"Tough situation!" he muttered.

I pretended to know nothing. "Why do you say that?"

"Maier two is an idiot! Got drunk and insulted the Führer."

"I heard him making a racket, but I didn't understand what he was saying."

"Lucky for you!" whispered the soldier. "They are putting all those who were around through an inquisition."

"Whom do you mean by 'they'?"

"Lieutenant Vogt and your party man."

"Nero?"

"I think that's what you call him."

"Has anyone informed against Maier two?"

"No, but your Nero seems to have heard something himself, though not very much. So they want to get it from others."

"And the others?"

The soldier shrugged. "The one who was drinking with Maier two is drunk himself. At least he acts that way; they can get nothing out of him. The rest insist that they heard some insults but understood nothing really. Maier two is a good guy. He has a family, wife and children, and in getting drunk — oh, well."

"What does he say himself?"

"Nothing — he's still drunk. The Lieutenant has him locked in the shelter. Man, I wouldn't want to be in his shoes tomorrow morning! I hope he doesn't remember anything."

"What does the chief say?"

"Vollmer?"

"Yes."

"He went to the city shortly after eight. A strategy conference or something like that. He won't be back until tomorrow evening. Vogt is taking his place. He's put Maier two under arrest for twenty-one days."

"They'll pass fast enough." I felt much better.

"Vogt has known Maier two a long time," the soldier continued. "It looks as though he wants to spare him the worst. The lieutenant's a regular guy."

"The worst? What do you mean?"

Instead of answering, the soldier drew his finger across his neck. "That, kid. Now go and report on your watch."

I hurried to the barracks and reported to Haberzettel.

"Get to bed," he growled. "No more gossiping, understand?"

A light was burning in the dormitory. Although my comrades were not asleep, none of them said a word. Haberzettel's orders had shut each mouth. A few minutes later he put out the light . . .

The next morning I met the soldier who had relieved me on the watch. "Your Nero went away last night," he whispered to me. "About eleven. He was wearing the party uniform. A third-battery man drove him on a motorcycle."

"Do you mean —"

He didn't let me finish. "No idea, and I haven't said a word, understand?"

At roll call I was still jittery when Haberzettel ordered "Attention!" and gave us a proper dressing down. He was fuming. At gun training nothing suited him. Lieutenant Vogt was not to be seen.

About nine o'clock the lightning struck. Nero was there, First Lieutenant Vollmer, and — a detail from the city! It was a clear day; from where we were drilling at the guns we could easily recognize the men.

"Keep on!" Haberzettel stormed at us, but I noticed that he, too, watched the shelter where the men had gone. It wasn't long before the detail reappeared. With Maier two! Vollmer and Nero remained in the shelter. Maier two walked with his head down, looking neither to left nor to right. They went off to the parking lot, and we heard the engine of a truck starting.

"They've arrested him!" Gerngross exclaimed.

"Swine!" muttered Haberzettel to himself, then turned to us and shouted, "You want to quit work, huh? Take full cover! — To the guns! — Take full cover! — To the guns! Before you kids came there was no pigsty to be got rid of! Take full cover! — To the guns!"

✠ 8 ✠

November, 1944

THE DAILY ROUTINE was always the same, and grew dull. This was a good thing. The more apathetic I became, the more fear vanished. Only on many a night dreams disturbed me. I saw and heard them: Maier two, Anna Thumser, Schroeder, Wittmann, Heller. They had the features of the Serbian, whose face I had looked at for only a moment. Then the horror would return, and I was afraid. Even an occasional night alarm was a relief!

Gerngross asked Haberzettel what would happen to Maier two. The corporal shrugged. "The chief will do what he can for him. Perhaps they will just assign him to another fighting unit. On the other hand — oh, forget it!"

In the camp Nero was surrounded by silence. Even Lieutenant Vogt cut him. We assistant gunners had to put up with him.

I received a letter from my father. He wrote that he was well and that he was sweating it out in his division.

The devil got loose on the night of November sixth. Enemy bombers again attacked our emplacement. I stood at the gun and held out until the end. Our barracks got a direct hit. Hauschild was killed, Schneider very badly wounded. Nero was on telephone duty — in the shelter, of course. We shot down two planes, one of them with my gun, and damaged others. After the attack and the cleaning up, we slept in tents. By a soldier who came back from the city, Mother let me know that our house had been somewhat damaged, that otherwise everything was all right.

On the afternoon following the attack, there was much commotion in the camp. Ten of the regular soldiers, this time younger men, were withdrawn. The word was that they were going to the western frontier of Germany, where an attempt was being made to hold off the assault of the Americans and English. From the city came a troop of Russian prisoners. They were put to work at once erecting new barracks and a second shelter, for us. Their guards were older soldiers who were fit only for garrison duty at home. Most of them wore the wound pin. They were as expressionless as the prisoners.

Nero kept a close watch on the Russians, subhumans as he called them, so that no one could give them food or cigarettes. It happened — in spite of him!

Toward evening we received reinforcements: twelve more girls of the auxiliary force, about seventeen or eighteen years old. They were to be trained as assistant gunners.

"I can't help laughing at them," grinned Barbarossa.

"Rubbish!" said Walter Müller.

The twelve were put into the first of the barracks built by the Russians, behind the officers' barracks. Vogt threatened to imprison anyone found strolling there.

On the morning of the ninth of November Lieutenant Vollmer made a speech before the entire battery. He talked of the National Socialists who, marching to their Field Hall in Munich on the ninth of November 1923, had been broken up by the guns of the regular army. Adolf Hitler was in the leading group of marchers. What would it have been like if a bullet had hit him? It frightened me that such a thought should enter my head. What a long way I had come!

In the afternoon the district director and the corps leader visited us. Wearing his brown party uniform, Nero gathered us assistant gunners in the classroom. The corps leader spoke to us of the dead Schroeder and Hauschild and held them up as examples which we should imitate. The district director spoke of Maier two as a traitor who had stabbed the German people in the back in the most difficult hour of their fateful struggle. Such people, he said, deserve to be eliminated. Both men congratulated me on the Iron Cross, Second Class. I gritted my teeth. . . .

In the evening I went to Point-five in his room. "Have you learned anything more about Mrs. Thumser, sir?"

"No, Briel. Only a few know what has become of her, and those few are silent."

"Concentration camp, sir?"

"Probably."

"What happens to the prisoners, Doctor? Are they forced to work hard or merely locked up?"

Point-five looked at me for a while, then he

answered. It was the first time that I had heard about the horrible things that went on in these camps. Slave labor — brutality — murders. Yet I had a feeling that Point-five was being merciful, that he was sparing me the worst. Also he was fair to those whose ideas he could not share.

"Not everyone who wears a brown uniform or the death's-head insignia is inhuman. There are party leaders and Home Defense soldiers who have managed to remain decent. Many of them vanish behind the same walls as the unfortunates who are branded as traitors or subhuman." He sighed heavily. "I am no friend of the enemy; they all accepted Hitler. They made diplomatic pacts with him and sent their youth to the Olympic Games in Berlin. They backed down when a clear No! should have been spoken. They sacrificed Austria and Czechoslovakia, thereby strengthening the Dictator's conviction of his invincibility. Now they are dropping bombs on our cities, not only on important military targets, but on the districts where women, children, and old people live."

He didn't need to say more; we understood each other. He did not believe in final victory, but he was ready to do his part in defense against the bombers. He was not fighting for the ideology which he would be glad to see destroyed, but for the fearful, the despairing, the helpless in the cellars of our city. Although he wore the party badge on his coat, he rejected what it stood for. He made me realize that the hanged Serbian and Maier two were not exceptions.

He was putting himself in my hands. If I said a single word to Nero . . . But he had no need to fear me. I was convinced. I asked him why I was the one in whom he confided.

He answered without hesitation: "One day we will no longer be firing at aircraft, Briel, but at ground targets, as they are so charmingly called. On tanks and jeeps with either red or white stars. Then the moment will come when, to avoid senseless shedding of blood, reasonable persons must stop fighting even if madmen would fight to the last ditch. I know you and your comrades, Briel; you are all my students. I have observed you carefully, and when you came back from your first leave in the city, I saw that you had been thinking hard. In our conversations after that I discovered how you felt. Since Bayer went into the hospital, I

151

have seen that your comrades listen to you. Briel, if worse comes to worst, you will restrain the boys from rashness and bring them through safely. You can speak convincingly when you must. You are all young and should survive!"

My head whirled. "Why did you join the party, Doctor?"

He did not take my question amiss. "I have been a party member since 1932. At that time I was twenty-one and like many others saw in Hitler the only man who could bring order out of the chaos in our country. He had promised to keep to democratic rules of the game. But the promise was not kept, and when my eyes were opened it was too late. I am no hero, Briel. I haven't the courage for open defiance. So I have kept aloof and attended only the public demonstrations and evening school sessions that I couldn't avoid without arousing suspicion. But my lack of zeal was suspected, and I was passed by when it came to promotions and appointments. As a hundred per cent National Socialist, I would have been a headmaster long before this. Now and then they have tried to set a trap for me and induce me to say something that would endanger me. I was careful — considered every word I spoke. Even in private conversation, especially with Dr. Ammon, I weighed every word. Should I have turned in the party badge?"

He didn't wait for my answer but gave his own. "I admire martyrs, Briel, but I am not of the stuff of which martyrs are made. However, I now see my duty. You and your comrades should survive, and you will help me to make it possible. Good night, my boy."

"Good night, Doctor, I — I thank you!" Our handshake was a promise.

In the days following I talked with Müller and Gerngross, at first cautiously, then more frankly when I found that Walter was open to being convinced. And he could be trusted to keep silent. Gerngross had long thought as I did.

Every so often the three of us went to see Point-five, slipping through the darkness like thieves. We were lucky; Nero never found out about our meetings.

To celebrate his fifty-fifth birthday, Nero canceled the Latin class and gave us a lesson in patriotism. He read the full report of the latest war news:

"In defending southeast Libau, the Fourth Regiment of Grenadiers under the command of Major von Bismarck distinguished itself by remarkable bravery. In the same combat area, Corporal Eil of the Fusileer Squadron alone repelled shock troops in close combat annihilating four encircling Russians with a grenade, which exploded and tore off his hand." Nero's voice droned on. "That is true heroism! An example to every one of you!"

"He should know," Gerngross whispered.

Nero saw the movement of the boy's lips but apparently had not made out the words.

"What did you say, Gerngross?"

"I said that it was an example, not only for us, but for all Germans."

"Of course, Gerngross, that is what I meant — I'll let you have the rest of the period. *Heil* Hitler!" He nodded and left the classroom. It looked like an escape.

Later, before the math class began, Point-five told us about the sentence passed on Maier two, of which Lieutenant Vogt had informed him. The corporal was demoted by the court martial to the rank of private and would be placed in a "disciplinary" company.

"What is that like?" Huber asked. We leaned forward anxiously.

"They do especially dangerous work: clear out mines, unprime dud bombs. Their casualties are extremely high. Now for today's lesson . . ."

The next morning brought a surprise. Nero had taken himself off! He said that he wished to take part in the fateful struggle of the German people in a different place. Therefore he had arranged to be sent to the eastern front for ground fighting.

"I'll eat a broom if it's true," Müller vowed. "Nero belongs in a place where shooting is done with words."

Gerngross put it somewhat differently. "He's going on account of Maier two, but he'll find a shelter wherever he goes."

After dinner the mail was distributed. I had a letter from Father, which had been almost a week in coming. From cautiously worded hints I knew that he was in the Libau danger zone.

About four o'clock a British reconnaissance plane — perhaps damaged — flew over our emplacement at a great height and did not attack us. We sent up some shells but didn't hit it.

In the days following, various work troops came into the vicinity of our camp: older men from the city who were drafted into this service because they were incapable of fighting at the Front, prisoners of war, and young boys from the labor service. They repaired streets, laid roads, built shelters, dug trenches. There was a great difference in their attitudes. Some were still enthusiastic, but they were a minority. Submission to fate and apathy were more common.

From time to time single sneak raiders appeared. We didn't score any hits. It would have taken shells whose flight path could have been controlled from the ground.

Corporal Haberzettel brought the latest newspaper from the city. It passed from hand to hand. Three pages were divided into small boxes decorated with the symbol of the Iron Cross. Death notices — names, names, names. First lieutenant — colonel — captain — sergeant — corporal — private first class — private. The greatest number were corporals and enlisted men. Killed in action in the west, in the south, on the eastern front, on land, on the sea, in the air. And under each notice the usual "In proud grief"; then the names of the bereaved. Some of them I knew. I knew Mrs. Hesse, a widow. Now her oldest son was killed in action on the eastern front "For Führer and country." "In proud grief: Marianne Hesse and son Gerd," I read. Gerd was not yet thirteen.

The newspaper lied! "In proud grief," the prescribed form, falsely proclaimed heroism where only despair existed.

✠ 9 ✠

Christmas, 1944

THE DESPATCHES brought news of heavy fighting in southern Belgium, near Aachen, in central Luxemburg, Upper Alsace, central Italy, Hungary, on the southern border of Slovakia, in Courland, and air attacks on western Germany, the Baltic region, and parts of south Germany. In the distance we could hear the detonation of bombs and the whistling of antiaircraft shells. But in our city and in our emplacement there was damnable, nerveracking quiet!

Only three of us had leave for Christmas. I was not one of them; we others were needed in the camp. But I could go home for New Year's. Too bad! I would so much have preferred the Christmas holidays.

In the classroom we had a little Christmas tree and an exchange of presents, which consisted mostly of alcohol. Point-five spoke about the message of Bethlehem, and we sang "Silent Night," not looking at each other.

During the following days there were no alarms. On New Year's Eve Gerngross, Braun, Müller, and I left the camp. The commander was very liberal; he gave us leave until four o'clock on the fourth of January, provided we did not get a sudden call to return.

Corporal Haberzettel gave us a hasty check before we left, and Point-five drove with us. He was going to visit a pensioned colleague. A truck took us to the city and dropped us near the school. As we separated, we wished each other a Happy New Year — "Better than the old," said Point-five.

It was cold, but the streets were clear of snow; only traces of white remained here and there on the walls of ruins, or rubbish heaps, or in odd corners. I met few people. They were in a hurry, seeming anything but festive. From a side street came a troop of prisoners of war — Russians. They trudged along as if pulled by strings. Only their eyes were alive. They were searching the road, perhaps for a crust of bread, a frozen potato, or a cigarette butt. Their guards looked sullen.

It was a relief to reach home. Mother expected me; I had sent word through a comrade that I would come home on New Year's Eve. She had succeeded in getting a piece of smoked meat on the black market. I didn't ask what she had exchanged for it. And of course I didn't come empty-handed. I had crisp bread, a little can of liver sausage, and a bottle of the French cognac which each of us had received as a Christmas present.

Mother showed me a letter she had received that morning from my father. He wrote that he was well and that we should not worry about him. "I expect to get leave in April at the latest," he concluded. The word "leave" was underlined. Mother and I knew he meant that the war would end by then.

We celebrated New Year's Eve by candlelight. The electric power supply was cut off again. It was to be used only in military emplacements and factories producing war materials. Our windows were blacked out. Mother had kept near her a little chest with the "shelter-pack," containing important papers.

At about ten o'clock the current came on again, so Mother turned on the radio. Soft music was being played. I hoped that it would not suddenly be interrupted by "Attention! Attention!" warning of the approach of a squadron of American or British planes. We let ourselves relax; still, each was aware of the apprehension of the other.

We spoke neither of the war nor of the future, but of the past. It sounded unreal, like the story of an unfamiliar world. That such things could be: clothes, shoes, food for money only — without ration stamps. Vacations in Switzerland, in France, and Italy. Concerts, the theater, dancing. Mother must have had a very happy girlhood.

The hours flew peacefully by. Shortly before midnight we prepared the New Year's Eve drink. I contributed the cognac, Mother the sugar, and there was plenty of water. At five minutes of twelve the music stopped. From the radio droned the voice of Propaganda Minister Goebbels, "Party and people! In these decisive —" Mother turned the radio off.

From a tower in the city we could hear a bell. We held our glasses and listened, then raised them in a toast: To Father — to the future — to peace. . . .

A little later some of the people in the house came in. The first was our air-raid warden. He was the type who liked to be top dog. He was a party member, block leader, an amputee of the Polish war, an enthusiastic Nazi. Nothing could shake his faith in the Führer. He made a speech about heroism, daring, and holding out to the end. For him they were not empty phrases; he believed every word. At the end he wished us a Happy New Year, and I clinked glasses with him even though I now thought otherwise than before. In spite of his fanaticism he was a decent fellow who had never done anything wrong and wouldn't hurt a fly. Yes, there are such people.

The others didn't talk so much. The women, with serious faces, pressed our hands, gave us their good wishes, and left. Afterward Mother and I drank the rest of the cognac and went to bed. I slept through the greater part of New Year's Day.

Shortly before noon the next day Mother went to the factory, where she worked the second shift. She took the little chest containing the papers with her, reluctant to part with it even when I was at home.

To pass the time I browsed among Father's books, listened to music on the radio, and finally lay down to sleep on the sofa in the living room. I wanted to stock up on sleep. Who knew when I would have another chance for a real snooze.

About half-past six in the evening the screaming of the sirens woke me. Air-raid alarm! I was more angry than frightened. Unwillingly I took my helmet and belt and left the room. In the hall I met some of the residents of the house who were not in any hurry to go to the cellar. Recently several alarms had been given merely as drills. Why should it be any different today?

When I reached the first floor the sirens had stopped. The air-raid warden urged us to move faster. It was mostly women with children who stumbled into the cellar. Many carried bed linen with them. I followed the air-raid warden outdoors and looked up at the dark sky. There were hurrying footsteps in the darkness and now and then a voice called a name. It was all very ghostly and I was not sure what to do.

Then — Ala-a-a-a-rm! The sirens screamed deafeningly. The warden seized my arm. "Get into the cellar! This is the real thing!"

I looked down into the cellar, saw the weak light, and suddenly felt that death was lurking there.

"Hurry up!" the warden urged me.

"Help!" a shrill woman's voice cried nearby, so loud that I heard it through the noise of the sirens. I ran in the direction it came from. Behind me the warden was still shouting. I didn't turn but hurried on.

Suddenly the city was lighted up by the searchlights, quickly followed by the barking of the antiaircraft guns. When I turned the corner, I saw the woman who had screamed. She was limping to the door of a house. "Are you hurt?" I asked, breathlessly.

She shook her head. "No, no, I'll be all right. I stumbled over a stone, fell, and hurt my foot. It's really all right, thanks very much. Be sure to go into the cellar." She disappeared into the house, and I stood alone on the street.

The antiaircraft guns were putting up barrage fire. There was a clattering sound as splinters of shell came down on the roofs. Then I heard the planes. The bursting shells of the antiaircraft guns increased to a heavy bombardment.

Where should I go now? Already I could hear clearly the whistle of an enemy reconnaissance plane. I shook off my numbness and ran inside the house the woman had entered, but then I was in darkness. I could not find the entrance to the cellar.

Back to the street! Not a soul to be seen and the only sounds the droning of the engines above me and the crackling of shells. Suddenly brightness! Stinging, painful brightness! The scout plane was dropping "Christmas trees" — dazzling magnesium flares on parachutes. Yellow, green, and red, they sank onto the roofs.

I ran to the house across the street as the roaring began which meant the arrival of the bomber squadron. I jerked to a stop, all at once relieved of fear. I knew where I belonged — at the guns! Instantly I took my bearings by the light of the parachute flares and ran. I must get to an antiaircraft gun site. I wanted to be in the fight.

In the center of the city the first bomb fell, and the sounds of crashing and screaming rose everywhere. Massive attack! Like a maniac I ran without any idea of where I was going. I thought no more about a gun emplacement or even of escaping into one of the houses. I just ran, ran, ran. . . .

Close behind me a bomb struck. The air pressure from the blast threw me into a bomb crater near the street. There had once been a green park here. I shook with the ground against which I pressed. The crashings, shrieks and blasts rose to an inferno of noise. Only after a long time did I dare to raise my head. The area which I could see from the bomb crater was not large, but even this bit of hell was hell itself. There was a steady rain of incendiary bombs, demolition bombs, and parachute mines. Houses flew apart, walls tilted and fell in on each other. Stones, clumps of earth, fragments of beams whirled through the air and fell down. The phosphorus of the incendiary bombs turned the city into a blazing torch. Now no more parachute flares were needed. Just in front of me a tree stump flamed, burned brightly, and went out like a match.

Then I screamed with terror. What looked like lava crept in a fiery torrent toward me. Phosphorus! I strained every muscle to leap out of the crater, and at that moment a stone crashed down on my helmet. When I came to some moments later, I saw flames and heard shrieks.

Above there was no droning of planes, around me no deadly roar; only the fire still blazing and the murderous heat which turned the city on a winter night into an oven.

My helmet had withstood the blow. The lava which had crept around me had found another outlet. Scarcely half a meter away from the edge of the crater it had drained into another depression. I had to pull hard to get my legs out of the rubble, but they obeyed me, and I stood up.

The wind carried a stinging smoke. Wherever I looked I saw fire. People were coming out of the cellars. Half-clothed, bleeding, with blackened faces, crying out when the phosphorus burned through the soles of their shoes. I cried with them; I had to give vent to my feelings. Then I ran madly, tripped over masses of rubble, got up again, my hands and knees bleeding, and kept on going, paying no attention to the hell raging around me. At last I was at home.

Dear God! Our house had been struck, and the cellar had not withstood the blow. The parachute mines had been stronger. Under the ruins no one was alive. Stinging smoke rose out of the debris; my eyes began to water. Paralyzed I stared at the picture of destruction. Someone pushed a shovel into my hands. "Get busy!"

The numbness went. I heard the noise around me and saw men with pickaxes and spades. I began to shovel like a madman, digging out the others in the rubble until I had no strength left. A short breathing space, then at it again. We salvaged some more or less damaged goods and — no! Where no help was possible one had to look the other way.

I started at the sound of my mother's voice. "My son!" She had come back from work at the usual time carrying her air-raid box. "You are still alive, Gustav," she said, unsteadily. "That's all that matters. Our factory wasn't hit." Then she got a spade and went to work.

A few hours after the attack the walls of the house fell in. Even in the morning Death demanded its victims.

All night fires blazed. The fire fighters were helpless. We worked until we were ready to drop, then the men of a new salvage troop sent us off.

Mother and I were in luck. We found a place to stay with a friendly family whose house had been only slightly damaged. I slept like the dead until Mother woke me at noon. The friends who had taken us in shared what little they had with us; we had saved nothing but the box with our papers and a crystal vase which I found intact in the debris.

Outside the noise of pickaxes, shovels and spades continued. So did the sounds of the clean-up machines which the bombs had spared, and that of the wheelbarrows and work carts which struggled through paths cleared of rubble, laden with damaged household stuff — and victims. Now and then we heard an explosion — a delayed action bomb. Soldiers and civilians rushed about in confusion: men in the labor service, Red Cross workers, the old, women, and children.

The owner of the house where we were staying told us that a parachute mine had fallen on the camp of the Serbian prisoners of war. More than thirty were dead and double that number wounded. At the height of the attack the antiaircraft gunners had to stop firing; they had no more ammunition.

When I went to the window, I saw the loudspeaker truck and heard the command: "All members of the armed forces stationed in the city and the environs proceed at once to your troop quarters."

Again we had to say good-bye. I stumbled along through the ruined city. Everywhere men were digging in the rubble: men with torn clothes, blackened faces, carelessly bandaged. Their grief was turned to stone; I heard hardly a whimper. Near where a salvage troop was working I saw a little girl about five years old sitting on a stone, hugging a singed puppet and smiling.

Of one church only the doorway was standing. The main part and the tower were a mass of fragments. Workers were clearing away the stones. Passing by I heard that people had run into the church when the attack came. They had run to death. In front of the portal a corporal was kneeling. He wore the uniform of the antitank troops. He had covered his face with his hands and did not move.

The stench of smoke was everywhere, and fires still smoldered in many places. Motorcycle despatch riders dashed along the cleared streets, conveying orders which could no longer be given by telephone since the network was broken. I hurried over to a cleared place and saw men, women, and children lined up before a field kitchen. Some organization or other was giving those hardest hit a warm meal.

A man with snow-white hair, his head bandaged, seemed to have lost his mind. "Dead! Everywhere!" he screamed. "Half the city is dead, and the rest of us won't live much longer!" Hardly anyone paid attention to him; they were interested only in the food being dispensed.

A motorcycle sputtered along and stopped near me. "Shall I take you part of the way?" the rider offered. When he got closer, he exclaimed, "Man, you're from our second battery!" I climbed into the sidecar.

"Were you in the city when it happened?" he asked. I nodded.

"Gosh, you were lucky!" and he stepped on the gas.

"What happened in the camp?" I yelled above the roar of the engine.

"Only a few bombs fell on us," he yelled back. "Some damage to the equipment and two dead, both of the second battery, Lieutenant Vogt and Assistant Gunner Korner."

We drove into the woods. How often in times past I had wandered with my father through the snowy forest; now too the pines were covered with hoarfrost, which glittered on the pine needles like silver. I didn't want to see it any longer. I closed my eyes.

Lieutenant Vogt and Karl Korner. We had called him the Bull.

Point-five and Gerngross came into the camp half an hour after me. They had survived the holocaust, but they brought bad news. Gerngross wiped his eyes as he told us, "Bayer is dead. Three hours before the attack he was in the hospital waiting to be certified as fit to return to duty. After the attack they pulled him out of the cellar where the ceiling had fallen in. I heard of it from an acquaintance."

Point-five gave us the second tragic story. Bombs had fallen on the military hospital to which the badly wounded Josef Schneider had been taken. The attendants did what they could, but the time between the alarm and the attack had been too short. Not all the wounded could be taken to

172

the air-raid shelter. Schneider was among those left behind. "It happened so quickly," Point-five tried to console us, "they could not have suffered."

Corporal Haberzettel sent us into the classroom. It looked so large that I felt lost. We were down to four! Alfred Schmidt, Manfred Huber, Gerngross, and I. Willi Braun and Walter Müller had not yet reported back from New Year's leave.

"A sad remnant of our gang," Huber tried to joke.

No one answered. Haberzettel and Point-five came in. We stood at attention, and Schmidt made the report. He still wasn't a real soldier. As he made his little speech, he seemed a one hundred per cent civilian. Haberzettel, who looked very tired, did not comment on this. "Lieutenant Vogt and Gunner Korner have been killed in action," he said hoarsely. "The chief has put me in charge of the second battery. You will have your regular duty at the guns. In the west, near Aachen, the enemy is on the German border. To block off the invasion or push back the enemy, all available reserves will be sent there. That means most of the regular soldiers here. They will go in the next few days. As substitutes we shall have more girls from the auxiliary, workers whose classification will be changed, and prisoners of war.

"As to the last attack on our city: Over a thousand British planes flew in concentric formation. The first estimates indicate that two thousand are dead and thousands wounded. — In ten minutes, drill at the guns! Break ranks!" He left with bowed shoulders.

Point-five nodded to us, muttered, "Chins up!" and followed the corporal. I saw him later training as a machine gunner.

Some days after the attack, we were ordered to the city for clean-up work. The batteries were manned by a skeleton force, since we did not expect an attack in the daytime. In the city the worst of the rubble had been cleared away. We relieved the exhausted men and women who had dug unceasingly in the ruins. Helpers also came from other gun emplacements. I saw many more men in brown uniforms now than I had before the attack. They encouraged the workers, issued commands, and cursed the "air gangsters."

During the noon hour I was able to visit Mother. She still lived with our friends and made no complaint. The munitions factory where she worked ran on an around-the-clock schedule now.

The newspapers gave the figures for the attack casualties: 1829 dead, 6000 wounded, almost 100,000 homeless. These last would be temporarily housed. Many of them lived in or under the ruins of their houses.

Mother had received no further word of my father. She was worried because Libau was not mentioned any more in the war dispatches. I tried to give her hope although my own heart was heavy.

On a Sunday in the middle of January a film detachment visited our position. In the classroom we saw the sound film *Hitler Youth Quex* which presented "the brave death of a German boy for Führer and party." At the end the political leader accompanying the detachment led in the singing of the Horst-Wessel song.*

Quex did nothing for me, and the Horst-Wessel song had lost its effect. Instead of joining in the singing, I just moved my lips in order not to be conspicuous. The political leader sang the loudest.

* Horst-Wessel was a young Nazi murdered by the Communists, made a national hero during the Hitler regime.

In the next two weeks nothing much happened. We carried out the usual routines under Haberzettel's command. Occasionally shells were fired against sneak raiders, but we suffered no damage. We were well trained now and needed no further instruction. The 8.8 had been entrusted to us.

Our battery now consisted of a motley crew. Men came from the city in the evening and went back in the morning. Huber called them moonlighters for the fatherland. They did not have an easy time: night guard duty, a few hours sleep, then back to important war jobs.

✠ 10 ✠

February 3, 1945

MY SEVENTEENTH BIRTHDAY. I spent it on weekend leave with Mother. Saturday morning she received a letter from the officer in command of my father's regiment, written almost four weeks before. First Lieutenant Hermann Briel had not returned from a shock troop operation, wrote the commander, but he had not been found among the dead. It was to be assumed that he had been taken prisoner.

"Missing in action!" Mother moaned.

How often I had heard these words. Yet only now did I realize their horror, now that my own father was listed among the missing. Missing in action! The suspense could not be more dreadful. Only the end of the war would bring certainty. Perhaps information from a prison in the east — from Leningrad, Moscow, Sebastopol, Ufa, Murmansk, Vladivostok. Russia was huge. It was no consolation to me that Father was one of many, like Walter Müller, who had not yet been found, vanished like Thumser's mother, who had been taken to an unknown place and gave no sign of being alive. . . .

Back at the emplacement, I talked with Point-five. "When the war is over, your father will surely come back," he said. For this "surely" I was grateful to him. Gerngross pressed my hand and said, "Others have it still worse, Gabriel."

Haberzettel had his own way of helping me. "Actually you were assigned to the watch, boy, but out there you'd only keep having stupid thoughts; so I'll assign someone else. Let's have a drink." He waved off my objections and shoved me into the classroom where we could be alone.

Haberzettel opened a bottle of schnapps which he had scrounged, heaven knows where. I was not accustomed to such strong liquor, particularly so much, but I drank it with him. The schnapps was effective; I heard myself talking and saw him nod. Then his face swam before my eyes — his head — his body . . .

The days and nights passed. Americans and British confined themselves to sporadic raids, and we began to hope that the attack on January second had been the last big one for our city. The blow which hit us unexpectedly came from the German side. Lieutenant Vollmer called together the whole crew of the battery and read this special proclamation:

Berlin, February 16. The Minister of Justice has issued the following decree concerning the establishment of courts martial:

The tightening of the ring around the country requires of every German the greatest war effort and devotion. Whoever seeks to evade his duty to the public, especially anyone who does this out of cowardice or self-interest, must be called severely to account so that the country shall not be shamed by the failure of a single person. It is, therefore, at the command of the Führer, in agreement with the Minister of State, the Head of the Chancellery, the Minister of the Interior, and the Leader of the party, ordered:

I. During enemy threats the State Defense Districts shall be drumhead courts martial.

II. 1. The courts martial shall consist of a criminal judge as chairman, with a political leader or organization leader of the National Socialist party and an officer of the armed forces, the Home Defense Staff or the Police as assistant judges.

2. The Commissioner of Public Safety will name the members of the court and appoint a Public Prosecutor to conduct the case for the State.

III. 1. The courts martial are courts of jurisdiction for all offenses by which the war strength or war spirit is endangered.

2. The procedure shall follow the regulations of the State Criminal Courts.

IV. 1. The courts martial may decree the death penalty, may absolve, or transfer to a regular jurisdiction.

2. The sanction of the Commissioner of Public Safety is necessary to set the place, the time, and the nature of an execution.

The chief made no comment. The prisoners of war in the camp had heard only the German text; nobody translated it for them since it applied only to Germans. The prisoners had been under martial law for a long time. I saw the chestnut tree behind the barbed wire. . . .

The chief granted us an hour of free time. Why and wherefore he didn't say. Gerngross and I strolled with Point-five through the woods while he explained the situation. In the west and east the enemy was on the borders of the country. Men who had been considered unfit for active duty and munitions workers, unfamiliar with the use of weapons, were being sent to the front. They were called "the People's Storm Troops" although they often wore only an armband on their civilian clothes. Their main weapon was the antitank bomb.

"So that's the secret weapon," commented Point-five bitterly. "Poor devils! They are nothing but cannon fodder. In front, the enemy; behind, the threat of court martial. Believe me, there will be many hangings in the last convulsions of the Thousand Year State!"

"Whoever endangers the war strength or war dedication is to be tried before the court martial," Gerngross quoted. "That can be interpreted as suits their purposes. Even a word spoken in despair or anger could bring one to the gallows."

"Not only could," answered Point-five. "It will!"

"I once said that I hated the murderers in the planes and whose who have got us into this mess," Gerngross recalled.

"The second part of your statement would be enough to get you hanged," Point-five declared.

"When I think that a few months ago I believed everything I heard in the Hitler Youth school and on the radio, and what I read in the newspapers, I could slap my own face!" I burst out. "They have themselves to blame that I have taken off the blinders — because of Nero, the man on the chestnut tree, Thumser's mother, Corporal Maier two, and much else which I saw and heard in the city."

"And because of me, Briel," said Point-five. "You may as well admit it! Gunners Briel and Gerngross and Instructor Winkler present three cases for court martial."

"Then thousands must be executed and tens of thousands imprisoned," I protested.

"Our prisons, penitentiaries, and concentration camps were filled to overflowing a long time ago," Point-five answered, "and if you think of the death sentences to be imposed after July twentieth, you can no longer really doubt that our government does not shrink from mass executions."

"The Führer is always right," murmured Gerngross. "Man, Gabriel, what idiots we were!"

I agreed. Then I had another thought. "If Nero were not at the Front, he would be appointed a member of the court martial."

Point-five corrected me. "Headmaster Ammon is not at the Front."

"He isn't?" Gerngross and I said together.

Point-five shook his head. "First Lieutenant Vollmer said at breakfast today that he had received a letter from a friend, a captain in some special service in the Bavarian Alps. Hardly an enemy plane, still less an enemy troop has ever gone astray there. In the letter it said that a certain Headmaster Ammon shortly before had been assigned to this service as an adviser. Vollmer gave no further details and made no comment."

"That sounds like Nero," Gerngross said. "Really we should have known he'd be doing something like that."

Point-five shook his head. "This is only clarification, to round out the picture, otherwise it's nothing. You know that I should like to assure your safety if the enemy invades our territory with ground forces. The establishment of martial law complicates everything. Spy troops of the party, of Home Defense, and military police will be on the watch for deserters. Take care not to become conspicuous. Leave all the rest to me. At the decisive moment I'll do whatever is possible. Next week I'll sound out Schmidt and Huber."

"And Corporal Haberzettel?" I asked.

Point-five smiled. "He is a simple man but a fine comrade. He knows what's going on and will put nothing in the way when the time comes."

We separated before going back to camp. Schmidt, Huber, and Haberzettel were in the common room. Huber asked, "Have you heard the newest joke? The quartermaster told it to me."

Haberzettel looked up. "Something political?"

"Rather."

"Then keep your mouth shut!"

For the next few days the camp seemed to be more peaceful. Here and there the few regulars remaining put their heads together and whispered, but stopped when the young ones passed them. Apparently they still thought us one hundred per centers and didn't want us to overhear them. The

184

court martial threw its shadow before it, even though the sessions had not yet started.

On the twentieth of February it was cold although the sun shone and the sky was cloudless. We ate at half past eleven because most of our company were to be driven to the city to a soldiers' theatrical performance. The poster announcing it hung outside our barracks, *Heaven, Arm, and Cloudburst.*

For once, something different! After dinner we dressed up, naturally, since the girls of the auxiliary were coming with us. We brushed our uniforms, gave our boots a brilliant polish, using up a lot of shoe cream and spit. Huber would not move away from the mirror. He was making a careful part in his hair.

Then everything changed. Just as we were about to set out — alarm! "Heavy enemy bomber squadron in flight over the city!" On a clear day!

"Muck!" growled Huber.

"To the guns!" shouted Haberzettel.

Right away we heard the deep rumbling; we were trained listeners. This time the planes were American. We recognized them from the roar of the engines even before we saw the white five-pointed stars on the bombers.

Barrage fire! The shells flew from hand to hand; I pushed them into the barrel. Point-five sat with a grim face at the sights of our 8.8. Bombs exploded in the city, then they started on us. Five — seven — ten — fourteen four-engined planes opened their bomb bays over us. We fired like mad. The bombers flew to a greater height, and the escort planes raked us with their fire. The ground shuddered under the bombs. I heard shrill cries. They could not come from the girls, who were in the shelter. They must come from the prisoners, who lay in the trenches since they were not allowed to fire the guns.

I felt no fear or anger, or despair. I felt nothing. I did what I had to mechanically. I was a gun loader, a robot; we all were robots, even Gerngross. He didn't panic, but toiled grimly.

A cone of fire crackled against the barrel of our 8.8. Someone near me shrieked, but I didn't turn. I felt only the shell in my hands. Then suddenly I grasped emptiness. "No more ammunition!" Huber yelled. We were helpless against the destruction raining down on us.

186

The bomber squadron drew off, looped, and came back. "Take full cover!" Point-five shouted. We couldn't reach the trenches, so we flung ourselves down just where we were.

An explosion near our 8.8 lifted the gun off its base. The air pressure picked me up and threw me two or three meters back, flat on the ground. Everything around me burned, crackled, trembled, burst. I clawed the earth and grabbed an arm near me. It was Point-five's; he lay bleeding from a wound in his forehead. "Quiet, Briel!" he cried. "Don't move!"

A roar overhead silenced us. A reconnaissance plane was rushing down, its gun spitting out streaks of light. Just in front of me the earth spurted up. But that was nothing. What froze me with horror was the tiger's head painted on the left side of the plane. It grew larger and larger. I pressed my face against the ground, felt dirt between my teeth, heard the thunder very close. Then I felt a blow, and nothing more.

When I came to, it was all over. The drone of the planes had died away in the distance. Point-five was trying to help me. His forehead was bandaged. "At last!" he said when I opened my eyes. I was lying in the open, but I wasn't cold; the Americans had taken care of that. There was fire all around me.

"Gerngross?" I asked wearily.

"Here," he answered from somewhere near me, and then I saw him. He was all right. "Haberzettel?"

"Had a narrow escape. He helped me raise the gun and put it back on its base."

"What good is that when we have no ammunition?"

"The chief has sent the last of the usable trucks to get some."

Before I could ask any more questions, Point-five spoke. "Schmidt has been killed, Huber badly wounded. He won't live through the night."

I wanted to get up but felt a sharp pain in my head and sank back. "That will pass," said Gerngross, trying to be gruff. "A bomb splinter hit your helmet." He bent and picked up a piece of steel as big as a hammer handle. "This was it, Gabriel, you were lucky!"

"Come on," Point-five called. "They need us."

I pulled myself together and stumbled after him and Gerngross. Gradually I estimated the extent of the devastation. Of all the guns in the emplacement only three could still be used, if we could get more ammunition. All the barracks were burned to the ground and the forest clearing had widened. The pines had burned like matches.

On the charred stump the remains of a poster still stuck, and some of the words were legible: Soldiers' Theater, *Heaven, A — A Farce.*

Our parking lot was completely destroyed except for one jeep and a truck. As for the men . . . The only people who had no injuries to complain of were the girls. The shelter had protected them. The worst off were the prisoners of war crowded in the trenches. The battery commander's sober announcement was that thirty-five per cent were killed. Point-five, Gerngross, and I helped to bury the dead. I looked — and looked away when I saw familiar faces.

Although Corporal Haberzettel was wounded, he got himself bandaged and refused to be taken to the hospital. So it was with most of the men who were not badly wounded. They stayed. It was not the threat of court martial which kept them there, but the comradeship, stronger than any command.

Toward evening the truck returned bringing

ammunition from the city. Vollmer laughed grimly. "Ten shells for each gun!"

"They'll leave us in peace for a while." Haberzettel was optimistic. "And if we demand ammunition every day, with luck we can hoard some."

The news the truck driver brought from the city was shattering. Roughly eight hundred bombers had flown over the city, and the attack had lasted one and a half hours. The electric and water mains in the south and west were destroyed; the railroad buildings were in complete ruins. All available auxiliary troops were employed, but they could not get the fire under control. The number of victims could not be reckoned. I trembled for Mother.

We toiled until late at night; even the girls worked with us. We didn't need the tents in order to sleep. While half of us kept guard and cleaned up the rubble, the others had a brief rest in the officers' shelter and in the one the war prisoners had built a few days before. Distinction of rank disappeared. Our truck and jeep were constantly in use. They took the badly wounded to one of the emergency hospitals in the city.

Corporal Haberzettel was wrong when he said

we would have a few peaceful days. They gave us no peace but came again on the twenty-first of February, shortly after eleven, even while the stench of the fires of the day before was stifling the city. The battery commander had to knock down a war prisoner to avert a panic. The poor devils acted like madmen.

We waited at the guns, a decimated battery — three guns and thirty rounds of ammunition.

Over a thousand bombers turned the city into a scene of chaos. We heard the roaring, screaming, bursting, crackling — and waited. Then the squadron circled and came over our emplacement. First Lieutenant Vollmer gave the order, "Open fire!"

I saw a four-engined plane go into a spin, with fragments flying off the right wing. Then — then lightning flashed, followed by an ear-splitting crash. Half conscious, I saw our 8.8 rear up. Done for!

I woke on a straw mattress in the shelter. Near me I heard the groans of those who, like me, were not severely wounded and therefore not admitted to the hospital where there was not room enough even for the worst cases. I had a concussion and a wound in my upper arm, caused by a splinter of metal from our 8.8. The pain was bearable. I would complain no more than Haberzettel. I would stay, in any case. Our battery now consisted of only one gun.

The commander, Corporal Haberzettel, Point-five and Gerngross were still alive. Gerngross came to see me and told me of the tragedies. Two girls were among the dead. They had been on their way to the shelter when the alarm sounded, but they didn't reach it.

After Gerngross, Haberzettel came. "Damn!" he growled angrily. "Our battery is officially liquidated. It doesn't exist any more. We are to go into the city, Briel, to strengthen the antiaircraft unit in the center. It has been hit harder than ours."

"Shall we stay together?" I asked weakly.

He shrugged, "God knows, kid. Just be glad you are alive."

✠ 11 ✠

The End of February, 1945

WE HAD BEEN TRANSFERRED to the city. Our emplacement was near the old imperial fort. It had been struck, but its thick walls had defied the rain of bombs better than houses could. Luckily, Point-five, Haberzettel, Gerngross, and I were together. We filled out the battery which was to assure the safety of the district leader's command post. This command post was a bomb-proof shelter of thick concrete and was not connected with the air defense. Point-five hit upon the reason.

"They are pulling us into the ground-fighting, Briel. It won't be long now."

I thought of the last army despatch, which reported battles in the Slovak mountains, in northern Silesia, in Goldberg, near Luban, Breslau, and Glogau, in West Prussia between Neustettin and Konitz — battles in the Tuchola Forests, west of the lower Vistula, and on the southern front of East Prussia. In the west, a ring had tightened on the Roer near Jülich, in the Eifel, and on both sides of Saarburg. The pincers were closing. Bombs were falling on Munich, Aschaffenburg, Linz, and towns on Lake Constance. The pilots of low-flying enemy planes even amused themselves by chasing individuals.

Point-five stayed with us willingly as a gun loader. I knew why . . .

Our new commander, a captain of antiaircraft artillery, gave me convalescent leave over the weekend. Later we would be assigned to salvage work; there were still many to bury. Day after day we took the dead out of the ruins; again and again dud bombs exploded and tardily claimed their victims.

I spent the weekend with Mother. The house in which she had found refuge had escaped the last bombing. We had much for which to be thankful in spite of all.

On Monday afternoon, during the last hour of my leave, the sirens screamed again. We hurried into the air-raid cellar. Nineteen people huddled together: three men, one an amputee soldier, six women, eight children, and I. The youngest child was only about six years old.

The door was shut; an oil lamp gave the only light. No one spoke, everyone listened. Even the children were quiet. They had old, wizened faces. The soldier held a little girl on his knee and kept stroking her hair. A young woman pressed her hands to her belly.

Then we heard the heavy attack and held our breath. All at once I felt a horrible fear. If the house crashed down on us — the cellar was not large. Even if the ceiling held, the air down here would soon be exhausted.

"No!" the young woman suddenly shrieked. "No — no — no!" She sprang up and stared with half-mad eyes around her. The air-raid warden tried to pull her back to her place. She pushed him away. "No — no!"

The smaller children began to cry. "Cellar phobia," muttered the soldier. I clenched my teeth and clawed at the box on which I sat. The young woman, with lightning swiftness, seized the heavy sledge hammer which was leaning against the wall and smashed at the door with full force. The wood splintered. Two men leaped to the aid of the warden. They wrested the hammer from her and dragged her back to her place.

The poor woman collapsed. "I am going to have a baby! Should it be born down here?" My mother took her in her arms. She spoke comfortingly to her and stroked the disheveled hair away from her forehead. Her sobbing became softer.

We weren't hit. The noise of the bombing came no closer and the sirens finally hooted the all-clear.

What followed in the next weeks was work-a-day routine. The People's Defense Troop was assembled. Men, mostly in the older age group, had to line up in the early hours on Sunday for military training. The city was to be defended to the last. "If we lose the war, I don't want to live!" a fifteen-year-old boy said to me.

I kept hearing about the arrest of slackers, propagandists, and deserters. The court martial imposed death sentences. The first victim was a Home Defense guard who was absent without leave to go to his family in the western section already occupied by the Americans. The second was a woman who gave refuge for a few hours to an escaped French prisoner. "Death by shooting."

Water and bread were scarce. The homeless people and the auxiliary troops warmed themselves at bonfires.

In our battery we carried on as usual; gun drill, sentry duty, military and political instruction. In addition there was salvage work, construction of rifle pits and antitank obstacles; practice in shooting with the antitank bomb. Point-five didn't bother Gerngross and me with math, but performed the same duties we did. We three communicated chiefly by glances. The party men made speeches to us soldiers and to the people in the city through loudspeakers.

Faster British bomber squadrons attacked on the sixteenth, seventeenth, and nineteenth of March. Incendiary bombs fell on the hospital, destroying the women's clinic with high-explosive bombs. Our defenses were almost powerless. The enemy squadron flew too high, and ammunition was scarce. In various air-raid shelters epidemics broke out, and there were no disinfectants. In spite of all this, the party leaders demanded continued resistance.

All the cynicism of the war revealed itself: churches, hospitals, homes, and historic buildings lay in ruins — and the munitions factory where my mother worked was undamaged. More and more women and children were victims of the bombing. I resolved to keep all this in my heart — if I survived — in order to shout it in the ears of those who would know the war only from hearsay — those born after it was over.

We had a three-hour noonday pause on the twenty-first of March, since we were nearly exhausted by so much salvage work. Point-five visited a friend; Gerngross stayed in the shelter of our battery to get some rest; I visited Mother. She had become thin and pale and coughed badly, but she was in good spirits. "We'll live to see the end of it," she declared.

"I hope so, Mother."

"I am certain, Gustav."

The time flew all too fast and once more we said good-bye. Mother embraced me. "God protect you, my son." I ran. If I was to get back on time, I had to hurry. We had talked too long, perhaps, and the emplacement was a good two kilometers distant from the house.

Less than two hundred meters from our battery a bulldozer pushed against a heap of rubble. Who could have guessed that a dud bomb lay under the debris? The flash and the explosion came just as I was climbing over a heap of stones in my path. I felt a pain in my temple and fell to the ground. Only a small splinter had hit me, hardly worth talking about, but I lost consciousness.

✠ 12 ✠

After Twenty Years

INCREDIBLE that already twenty years have passed! It seems to me that I can feel the splinter still in my temple. But no, I am writing on Saturday, October 3, 1964. I have tried to think again the thoughts of Gunner Briel. I have not been wholly successful, I know; the thoughts of a man thirty-six years old have overlaid the earlier ones. What does it matter? The substance is there. I am thankful that I survived even if I did not reach my goal.

The splinter was to blame for that. They worked over me for two years; then it took more time before my brain functioned completely. After that it was too late for me to go back to high school. I became an apprentice, then a worker, and I am content. My mother survived, too, with her little box.

200

We endured the American occupation and the separation of the two Germanys. I live in West Germany. Haberzettel is over there in East Germany. He is a porter in a people-owned factory. At Christmas and Easter we exchange greeting cards.

My father did not come back. Until her death three years ago, Mother hoped for his return; I did not.

Thumser's mother was presumed dead. He recovered from his wounds and became a doctor. Willi Braun was never heard from again after the New Year's bombing.

Walter Müller reappeared after the Americans took over. During the last part of the war he had succeeded in keeping himself hidden. Now he is teaching German and history in the same school that we attended. We have often spoken of Point-five and of what a good man he was. Gerngross has him to thank for his life. When the Americans advanced toward our city, Point-five took Gerngross through the lines. He signaled to an American armored scout tank, but the soldiers suspected a trap. A machine gun struck Point-five down, but Gerngross was not hit, and the Americans let him escape. Today Gerngross prays for his rescuer, for the victims of the war, and for peace. He has become a monk.

In a little village in Upper Bavaria Nero lives on his pension, trying to forget the past. He has withdrawn almost completely from the public eye since his release from an internment camp. How does he really feel? I am no clairvoyant. . . .